THE
BRIDESMAIDS

BOOKS BY VICTORIA JENKINS

The Divorce

The Argument

The Accusation

The Playdate

The New Family

THE DETECTIVES KING AND LANE SERIES

The Girls in the Water

The First One to Die

Nobody's Child

A Promise to the Dead

THE
BRIDESMAIDS

VICTORIA
JENKINS

Bookouture

Published by Bookouture in 2022

An imprint of Storyfire Ltd.
Carmelite House
50 Victoria Embankment
London EC4Y 0DZ

www.bookouture.com

ISBN: 978-1-80019-976-7
eBook ISBN: 978-1-80019-975-0

NOW

SUNDAY

'Wake up! Wake up!'

Someone is shaking her arm. God, her head hurts. She tries to open her eyes but she can't at first, a searing pain at the front of her brain keeping them closed. Her arms and her legs and her brain hurt, and everything aches as though her body weighs a tonne, and... Oh God. What happened last night? What has she done?

'You need to come downstairs. Come on!'

She can hear crying. It pierces the room like the sound of a newborn, but there are no children here. She shouldn't have come away this weekend. She shouldn't have drunk so much. Someone is crying. She needs to make it stop.

Last night begins its gradual creeping return, an assassin in waiting. The party, the drink, the blackmail, the drugs, the photograph, the arguments... they each come back to her in turn, the memories too vivid and too real. Irreversible.

The pool. Oh God... the pool.

The grip on her arm tightens. Mumbled words, something about the police. The raging hangover that rips through her brain reduces the noise of everything else, as though the talking, the tears, the panic that is escalating on the ground floor might be muted for a while longer until she's ready to receive them.

But she'll never be ready for this.

She allows herself to be half dragged from bed, the cold hand closed around her bare arm, and now she realises that it isn't morning, it is still dark. A hen weekend, but this is no party; they are stuck in a nightmare, and she knows before she gets down the stairs where she is being led to, because she has already seen it for herself, last night, before she fled like a coward and tried to drive from her mind the horror of what had happened.

When they get there, the room is bathed in a soft glow of purple lighting that reflects off the water. Beyond the bifold doors, a wall of darkness stares back. Less than forty-eight hours ago, the stretch of open field beyond those doors and the wall of woodland that surrounds it made her feel as though they had reached a blessed corner of the earth, cut off from the rest of the world and from the lives they had left at home. It was a good feeling, a temporary escape from the chaos and the rush, and yet now it seems they are stranded here, trapped within this nightmare.

She focuses on the twinkling stars set within the ceiling above the pool – anything to avoid having to look at the heart-breaking scene that lies before her.

'Help me... I don't know what to do. Should we move her? I've called the police.'

The crying from the corner of the room intensifies. She has to force herself to look at the water. She is face down, submerged, arms splayed; hair fanned beneath the surface, morbidly beautiful. Ophelia. Her robe, weighted with water, is gathered at her waist, exposing her thighs, and she feels an unsettling urge to get into the pool and cover her.

'Say something! Please!'

She can't think straight. She doesn't know what to do.

Behind them, a single scream splits the room.

She can't turn to its owner; she can't be expected to be the one who should know what to do, not when one thought has destroyed the possibility of any other. The thought that she is responsible. She killed her.

THIRTY-EIGHT HOURS EARLIER

ONE

Holly

'What time is Claire picking you up?' Aaron asks.

I glance at the clock on the kitchen wall. 'Half an hour.' A mystery weekend away, the company of friends; the chance to do and think about nothing other than relaxing. At least that's what I'm hoping for. With Martha having appointed herself party planner, who knows what might happen. Whatever awaits me, though, I'm already grateful for it. Time and effort have gone into preparing for this weekend, and with everyone's lives as busy as they are, it can't have been easy to make arrangements. Finding an opportunity when we're all available at the same time usually proves difficult enough on its own.

'What am I going to do with myself all weekend?' Aaron muses, tapping idly at his laptop. 'Impromptu house party? Couple of triathlons? Netflix binge? The possibilities are endless.'

'You could finally get around to clearing out the shed.'

'I don't think I'll be that bored.' He flips his laptop closed and gets up from the table, where the tea he made me has gone cold. My stomach can't seem to handle anything this morning. I didn't sleep well last night. I was woken by Joseph, his presence so tangible that he might have been standing beside the bed looking over me. He is always here, but just recently – ever since the wedding was booked and the invitations sent out – he is with me more often, as though he doesn't want to let go. As though he believes that I am abandoning him, and he's not ready for it to happen. I couldn't stay in bed, not while the memory of him was so alive and present, so I came downstairs to the living room, where I sat in the darkness, never quite alone.

He wouldn't want you to spend the rest of your life on your own. If I had a pound for every time those words have been spoken, I could afford to leave my job at the surgery. Claire has said it, Martha has said it, even Caleb has said it, though he was too young when his father died to remember him or to know what he might have wanted. This morning, for a brief moment, I forgot my guilt. And then I saw my son. He was standing in the kitchen, scrolling his phone as he waited for his porridge to ping in the microwave. It could have been his father standing there, just as he was all those years ago, the similarities between them so striking that I was transported to another life, a teenager again.

Aaron's hand rests on my shoulder and he squeezes it gently. 'Relax. Enjoy yourself. You deserve this.'

As though he has read my mind. He seems to know when I need reassurance, and this is one of the things I love about him, one of the reasons why he has stayed in my life for far longer than any of the few men I have known since Joseph. Of course, I could never tell him that I was awake half the night thinking about the man I might already have been married to if things had happened differently.

'Remind Caleb about his interview tomorrow, won't you?' It's just a part-time job at a local pub, but Caleb needs to get himself organised or there will be no work still available by the time his exams end. When he leaves for university in September, there may be a chance for him to get transferred to another pub with the same brewery, so I'm hoping he'll take it seriously and make sure he gets there on time. He's already had to repeat a year of college because he spent the last one messing about. 'I've ironed him a shirt,' I add, gesturing to the utility room.

I haven't told Aaron about the drugs I found in Caleb's college bag last week. I've spoken to Caleb about it, I'm dealing with it, and I trust that my son will make the right choices in future. The wedding is less than a month away, and I don't want to worry Aaron with anything in the build-up to it, especially not with things that are my responsibility. But my son's stupidity grates, and I'm trying not to let it set the wrong tone for this weekend.

Aaron leans forward, his lips against my ear. 'Stop worrying. Everything will be fine.' I turn to kiss him, but we are interrupted by the doorbell.

'That'll be Claire. Have a good weekend.' We kiss goodbye. 'See you Sunday.'

Claire is waiting at the car, boot open and waiting for me to put my things in.

'All set?' she asks.

At the sight of her case – large enough for a fortnight's holiday abroad – I wonder whether I've packed enough. 'I thought we didn't need very much? Martha said we're not really going out anywhere, just to bring a dress for tomorrow night.'

'Ignore me. I'm used to packing with three small children in tow... over-preparation is a habit now.'

'So that's a suitcase of nappies and wet wipes, is it?'

'You have everything you need,' Claire instructs with mock sternness. 'Now get in.'

In the car, I put the postcode Zoe gave me into Claire's sat nav, for an address in Lawrence Hill, on the other side of Bristol. Claire is quiet as she drives and there are things I want to ask her; things I won't be able to mention once Zoe is with us.

'Are you okay?' I say.

'I'm fine. Really looking forward to this weekend.' She is evading the subject, knowing what I'm referring to.

'The thing with Gareth—'

'Everything's fine. Honestly.' She turns to me and smiles, as though this alone is confirmation of just how fine she is. We both know it's a pretence, although we haven't been able to talk about things as much as perhaps she needs to. She keeps saying she's been too busy with the kids to meet up, although sometimes I think she's using them as an excuse to avoid seeing me and having to talk about what's been going on. Maybe she's worried that if she reveals too much, I'll find out just how bad things have really become.

'You know if you ever want to talk about anything...'

'I know,' she says, moving a hand to my knee. 'But not now, Hol. This weekend is all about you, okay?'

When we reach Zoe's street we are greeted by three teenagers taking a joy ride on a shopping trolley, two travelling together, wedged side by side, while the third pushes, sprinting down the road as though he's about to propel his friends down a bobsled course. The trolley misses the front of the car by inches, and the boy shouts something and flicks a V at Claire as though the near-collision was somehow her fault.

'Idiot,' she mutters.

'Here,' I say, gesturing to one of the houses.

She pulls over at the kerb. 'I didn't think Zoe lived around here.'

'She's back living with her mum. Split up with her boyfriend and couldn't afford the mortgage on her own.'

A moment later, Zoe appears at the door. She looks gorgeous – dark hair piled high on her head in an effortless way that probably took far longer than it looks, and a smart navy trench coat that cinches in her waist – and I instantly feel that I should have made more of an effort. I have dressed for comfort rather than style today, the forecast saying there's a possibility of snow later on. Zoe and I have rarely been out anywhere together; she is ten years younger than I am, and work nights out have never really been much of a thing. Our friendship exists within the four walls of the surgery reception area, and now I wonder how the dynamic over the weekend will work and whether she'll fit in with the rest of our group.

'Hi,' she says, getting into the back seat. 'Thanks so much for picking me up.'

Claire and Zoe have met a couple of times before, when Claire has brought her children to the surgery.

'Do you know where we're going yet?' Zoe asks me.

'No idea. But we're under instructions to meet at Martha's first.'

We head towards Bristol's harbourside, for what Martha has described as pre-party drinks at her waterfront apartment. Both Claire and I know that what this really means is that she would like us all to see her new bespoke kitchen, and we're happy to humour her enough to delay the start of the weekend by an hour or so. Two of us will need to drive to wherever it is we're heading after that, so Claire and I have already agreed to use the unfairness of alcohol exclusion as an excuse to get moving as soon as the fittings have been admired.

Martha lives in an exclusive development overlooking Bristol Harbour, where a two-bed apartment costs in excess of half a million pounds. After her mother died when she was just thirteen, Martha's father sold the family home in Saltford and bought a dilapidated farmhouse that he renovated and sold for more than five times the purchase price. Twenty-five years on, he has a portfolio of over four hundred rental properties, and Martha is employed by his company.

'Wow,' says Zoe, as Claire pulls into the private car park. 'This must have cost her a bomb.'

'Cost Daddy a bomb,' Claire mumbles.

We go up to Martha's second-floor apartment in the lift, and she meets us in the doorway looking as though she is already dressed for the wedding. Despite the cold weather, she's wearing a short dress that accentuates her impossibly long legs, bare and tanned; the neckline that rises beneath her chin manages to make her appear even taller.

'Wow,' Zoe says. 'Amazing dress.'

'Thanks,' says Martha, and I cast Claire a wry smile. Martha is going to love unsuspecting and admiring Zoe. With any luck, she can be treated to an exclusive tour of the new kitchen while Claire and I hide somewhere and wait for Toni and Suzanne to arrive.

We follow Martha into the apartment, where a tray of glasses and an open champagne bottle await us in the hallway. Everything Martha does is planned with precision, which can be both a blessing and a curse. I admire her meticulous attention to detail, though it has often meant spontaneity is out of the question. It does, however, mean that nothing is left to chance, and that every get-together with her is regarded as an 'experience'.

'We could wait for the others,' she says with a shrug as she reaches for the bottle, 'but there's plenty more where this one's come from.'

She fills a glass and passes one to me, then one to Zoe.

'Are you sure you don't mind driving, Claire? I'm more than happy to if you've changed your mind.'

'You only have two seats,' Claire replies, a little too bluntly.

'Two of us in mine, four in Toni's. It's doable.'

'It's fine. I'm happy to drive.'

Zoe glances past Martha into the open-plan living space at the back of the apartment. 'This place is like something out of a magazine.'

'Thanks. Come on through.'

We follow Martha to the kitchen, where she gets Claire a glass of orange juice. She manages to hold back mention of the new kitchen until Zoe passes comment on the worktop, but soon after she begins discussing it, she's interrupted by the buzzer. She heads into the hallway to let Suzanne in, and while she's gone, I check my phone. I have a message from Toni.

'Something's happened with Georgia,' I tell the others when Martha returns with Suzanne. 'She's running late.'

Martha hands Suzanne a drink while I introduce her to everyone. 'To the weekend,' Martha says. 'And to the gorgeous bride-to-be.' She smiles and raises her glass to me. I take a sip before texting Toni back.

What's happened? Is everything okay?

'What's going on with Georgia then?' Martha asks, her voice devoid of any real concern.

'I don't know, she hasn't said.'

A few moments later, Toni's name lights up my screen, and I go into the hallway to answer her call. 'Is everything okay?'

'I'll be outside Martha's in five,' she tells me. 'Could you meet me in the car park?'

'Yeah, sure. I'll head down there now.'

Toni arrives with her daughter in the passenger seat. Georgia is wearing an oversized hoodie that manages to partially cover her face, and her long legs are raised, feet resting on the dashboard, head turned so that I'm unable to see her. Toni parks the car and gets out. She looks flustered, her blonde hair pulled back into a messy knot and a smear of what looks like some sort of dough on her sweater. She's as close to tears as I have seen her.

'What's happened?' I ask. 'Is Georgia okay?'

'No,' Toni says, though she offers no clue as to what is wrong. 'You won't believe what she's gone and done this time.' She sighs. 'I'm really sorry, Hol. I'm not going to be able to come. She's in such a state... I can't leave her when she's like this.'

'Don't worry.' I'm disappointed, of course I am – along with Martha and Claire, Toni is one of my oldest friends – but whatever is going on with Georgia, family comes first.

'I've got something in the boot for you.' She goes back to the car and takes out a box. 'Don't open it until you get there, okay?'

'Pinky promise,' I say, trying to sound light-hearted. 'Thank you.' I glance at the passenger window. Georgia has turned now, her make-up-smudged eyes focusing on her phone. 'Is she okay?' I ask again.

'You know Georgia. She's a constant worry. I'm so sorry. You understand, don't you?'

I want to ask again what's happened, but if she hasn't already told me then it's unlikely she's going to; not here and now, at least. 'Of course I understand.'

She looks gutted, torn between motherly duties and the prospect of a break from normal life. We have been looking forward to this weekend for so long. It's been an excuse for us to all get together and catch up – something that is well overdue.

'Could you bring her with you?'

Toni looks surprised by the suggestion. 'I can't do that. I mean, thank you, but she hasn't got anything with her, and anyway, I doubt she'd want to come, not when she's like this. And look at the state of me,' she adds, gesturing to her clothes. 'There was a problem at the bakery – I haven't had a chance to go home and change yet.'

'There's still time for you to get ready.'

She deliberates for a moment. 'Is there even room for Georgia? There may not be enough beds.'

'I'll check. I'll sleep on the sofa if necessary – I'd rather you were there. I can't have one of my bridesmaids missing, can I?'

Toni bites her lip. 'I don't know. Martha's not going to be happy about it.'

'Don't worry about Martha – I'll deal with her. Speak to Georgia. See what she thinks. She doesn't have to be with us all the time if she doesn't want to, but at least you can be there when she needs you.'

She goes back to the car, where Georgia is now scrolling her phone. She has been crying, her cheeks red and blotchy and her eyes smeared with dark make-up. I see her shake her head in response to Toni's words before looking at me, her expression somewhere between contempt and pity, difficult to decipher. I don't want her coming away for the weekend any more than Martha will, but I'm a mother too, and I get it. Georgia is emotional and unpredictable at the best of times, and I know Toni won't leave her on her own when she's vulnerable.

'Are you sure about this?' Toni asks when she eventually returns.

I get the impression it has taken some persuasion to get Georgia to agree to come. 'Absolutely.'

'You're the best, Holly, you know that?'

I shrug casually. 'Yeah, I have been told.'

Toni smiles and reaches to hug me. 'Thank you.' When she pulls away, there is something unsaid in her eyes, an alien look that leaves me strangely cold for a moment. 'I mean it... thank you.'

'It's nothing,' I tell her. 'Just give me five.'

I go back up to the apartment to let the others know about the addition to our group. 'Georgia's coming with us.'

Martha's hand rests on the fridge as though she's just been

doing a *Price is Right*-style presentation, her perfectly mani-cured fingernails flashing rose gold against the chrome handle. 'You're joking, right?'

'It's the only way Toni can come. She can't leave Georgia in the state she's in, can she?'

'Course not,' Claire says.

'Oh for fuck's sake,' Martha mutters. 'Do we even know what's wrong with her? Boyfriend's dumped her? Instagram gone down for an hour?'

The rest of us fall into an awkward silence. Martha can be bitchy when she wants to be, but her good qualities outweigh her sometimes brittle nature.

'It's not ideal, I agree,' I say, trying to pacify her. 'But it is what it is. If we want Toni there, we have to take Georgia. Anyway, she'll probably stay in her room most of the time.'

'She may as well stay home then,' Martha retorts. 'She's eighteen, for goodness' sake, not seven.' Her lip curls. 'Okay, whatever.' She sinks the last of the champagne from her glass. 'Let's just get going then, shall we?'

TWO

Claire

We drive for what feels like forever. The lanes are so narrow that at one point I start to wonder whether we'll all end up having to get out and walk. A nightmare for Martha in the shoes she's wearing. It's only an hour from her apartment – about three miles from the village of Calne – but the place feels remote and isolated. Other than Holly, we have all seen photos of the house before today, shared to the group chat I set up after Holly sent me the names of the people she wanted here this weekend. The final decision over the accommodation landed with Martha, of course, who appointed herself party planner before a hen weekend had even been mentioned; still smarting, no doubt, from the fact that she hadn't been asked to be maid of honour.

Once we pass through a huge set of gates that appear from nowhere along the lane, a wide expanse of space greets us: vast lawns and massive oaks set within an enclosure of woodland;

the converted barn at the heart of the retreat. Though the place looked incredible online, the photographs didn't do it full justice. The grounds and the barn are like something from a film set. I hate to admit it even to myself, but Martha has chosen well. No doubt she'll be smug as hell about it all weekend.

'Oh my God,' says Zoe, leaning forward between the seats. 'This is amazing.'

Wondering whether she has any other adjectives in her vocabulary, I park the car at the side of the barn, where there is enough space for at least five vehicles.

'Let's pick our rooms before the others get here,' Martha says, still annoyed by the change in plans and by Georgia crashing the weekend. We've still no idea what's wrong with her, but if it's enough to make Toni want to keep her close then it must be something serious.

We access the key to the barn with a code Martha got from the owner, and when we let ourselves in, we are greeted with a bottle of champagne and some chocolates left in a basket on the hallway table. Everything is made of solid oak, from the huge front door to the grand staircase. The ground floor has an enormous living room, with grand chandeliers hanging above three huge sofas, and the open-plan kitchen diner has a wall of bifold doors that open out onto a patio area.

We check out our surroundings, marvelling at the grandeur of the place, while Martha assesses the finishes as though she's preparing a planning spiel to be delivered to potential buyers.

'Look at this,' Zoe calls from the kitchen, gesturing to a door she holds ajar. We follow her down a darkened corridor and emerge at the other end in a separate building where the swimming pool and spa are housed. We've already seen this on the website, but it's even more impressive than the photographs could convey. Holly laughs with disbelief as she surveys our surroundings. I wait for Zoe to comment on how amazing it is, because it really is. I have never stayed anywhere like this before; I've never been able to afford to. The thought jars, ruining the moment. We paid just over a couple of hundred pounds each for this weekend. There are only six of us. It must have cost so much more than that.

'We'd better go and check out upstairs,' Martha reminds us, still keen to get the pick of the bedrooms.

The biggest and best of the rooms goes to Holly, who told us before coming here that she would share with Suzanne as no one else has met her before. I was supposed to be sharing a room with Toni, but now that Georgia will be here with us, that plan has changed. I don't think sharing with Martha will be a good thing for either of us, so I settle with Zoe, leaving Martha with a room to herself. For all her complaints about Georgia coming with us, this at least has worked out well for her.

The others arrive while we are upstairs, and we congregate in Martha's room. Georgia stands by the door and scrolls her phone, making no attempt to engage with any of us.

'I've got something for us,' Martha says, and she pulls two large gift bags onto the bed. In them are six white boxes with our names on. She hands them to us in turn, watching as we remove soft white robes from their tissue paper.

'Team Bride,' Holly says, reading the lettering on the back of her personalised robe. 'Thank you so much, Martha. These are beautiful.'

Beneath the robe is a pair of slippers, again personalised, and a keepsake compact mirror engraved with the hen party weekend dates. Thoughtful, I think. No expense spared. A shiver of resentment snakes through me.

'I didn't know you were coming, Georgia.' Martha looks at Georgia, who says nothing until Toni raises her eyebrows as a prompt.

'Don't worry,' she mumbles, coerced into a response, before rolling her eyes and returning her focus to her phone.

The others utter thanks, and I join them reluctantly. We

weren't told about these, and I wonder how much they set Martha back. Not that it would have set her back exactly. Whatever the cost was, it was likely to have been a minuscule drop in a vast ocean, and Martha has always been keen to flash her wealth as an opportunity to impress.

First the cost of the accommodation, and now these. I make a mental note to look back at the link for this place later and try to find out how much it has really cost. I wonder whether Martha has any idea what a teaching assistant's salary looks like. She has obviously subsidised us all on the cost of this place, and why would she do that other than to try to impress Holly with the grandeur and luxury of a weekend she will take all the credit for? This isn't about Holly, not really. It is all just a competition.

'Shall we all get ready?' Martha suggests. 'I can hear that sauna calling my name.'

Back in the bedroom, I check my phone, wondering whether Gareth might have texted me. I have no signal. It's the boys' bath time, though I wonder whether he will bother with it on a Friday evening. The kids are probably sugar-high by now, bouncing off the walls of the living room, making the most of being able to run riot in my absence.

Give the boys a goodnight kiss from me, I type, but when I try to send it, it doesn't go anywhere.

I catch a glimpse of Zoe in the mirror of the en suite, perfect in her bikini. She makes me feel old and frumpy, self-conscious in my maternity swimsuit that still fits me better than it should. My youngest son is four years old, plenty enough time for me to have got back into shape, so every health magazine and online fitness blog reminds me. But no matter how unhappy I might be with myself, I just don't have the time or the motivation to do anything to change.

'Ready?' She emerges from the en suite wrapped in the robe Martha bought her. I would like to say yes, but the truth is that I wish the weekend didn't involve us all having to be half dressed. Already knowing the rest of the group to be slim and attractive, I was hoping that Suzanne might be a little softer, a little rounder around the edges – a bit more like me. Instead, she is slim, and there is something too try-hard about the way she styles her hair and the clothes she wears; something that might make another woman look glamorous but manages to make Suzanne look older than I know she is.

'I just need something from Toni,' I lie. 'I'll see you downstairs.'

I tap at Toni's door. 'Where's Georgia?'

'Gone to the car for something. Did you know about these?' She gestures to the robe she's wearing.

'No. I wanted to ask you the same thing.'

She goes to the bed and picks up the box. 'I wonder how much they cost,' she says, before digging around in her bag for her phone. 'I wish she'd mentioned it. I don't want to be in anyone's debt.'

She sits on the edge of the bed as she taps the company name into her search engine. I notice a tremor in her hands.

'You've got internet then?' I ask her, pulling my attention from her fingers. 'I can't even send a text.'

'It's a bit on and off.'

I wait while she tries to match the items, wondering for a paranoid moment whether Holly might have said something. The reference to debt was just a passing comment, I know that really, and yet it felt so specific. But I trust Holly. I've talked to her in confidence, and I know she would never betray that.

'Bloody hell.'

'What?'

'Sixty-five quid a box. Almost four hundred quid! I know it's spare change to Martha, but it's not to the rest of us, is it?'

I shrug. Though we are all light years away from earning Martha's income, Toni is far from struggling. Her Bristol bakery has been a continued success since opening over ten years ago, and she was recently awarded South-West Wedding Cake Designer of the Year by *The Bride Guide* magazine.

'She should have asked us first,' I say.

'It's very generous of her.' Toni pauses. 'As always.'

She turns away from me, her face hidden as she returns her phone to her bag. I wonder whether her words said more than was intended, and a pang of guilt stabs at my side. Martha *is* generous; she always has been. It's just hard to ignore the way it can sometimes make the rest of us feel. We will never be as successful as she is. None of us will ever be quite as *able*.

'Are you okay?' I ask. Toni's eyes are watering. She never cries, and I don't want her to start now, not while the two of us are alone like this.

She nods but says nothing, though it looks as though she is holding something back, something she tries to swallow down before it can escape.

I open my mouth to speak, but my words aren't given chance to form. Georgia bursts into the room, her hair damp against her head and her face flushed pink with the cold. 'It's snowing,' she says impassively.

'Where have you been?'

'Trying to get a signal. I thought this place was supposed to have free Wi-Fi?'

'I can't get a signal either,' I say.

'There are taps shaped like swans in the downstairs bathroom,' she continues, ignoring the fact that I've spoken, 'but they can't sort out their Wi-Fi? Pathetic.'

She throws herself down on the bed and thumbs her phone screen. Toni rolls her eyes and looks at me apologetically. Georgia has barely spoken to anyone since we got here, spending most of her time wandering around the grounds trying to find a signal. I can only presume that whatever is so urgent must relate to the drama that has brought her with us this weekend, and I see Toni eye her with an unashamed contempt. Does she resent having brought her here?

'Are you coming downstairs?' she asks her daughter.

'No.'

She clearly wants to say more, but she holds back whatever it is, presumably because I am here. I dread the boys' teenage years if this is what they'll be like; I've heard boys can be easier than girls, but whether that's true or not, I'll have to wait to find out. Georgia has always been complicated; she was like it even as a young child, always hanging from her mother and making constant demands. The rest of us used to assume that it was because she had only ever had Toni to depend upon and turn to. She relies on her for everything, but there are times she can be horribly disrespectful to her.

'We'll be in the spa if you need us, okay?' Toni turns to me with a smile that is clearly forced. 'Shall we go?'

Once we're on the landing and the bedroom door has closed behind us, I get a chance to ask her what she was about to say to me before Georgia came in. She shrugs off the question. 'It was nothing, honestly.'

But her eyes are still glistening with the tears she's held back, and I don't believe a word of it. My raised eyebrow tells her so. 'Is it about Georgia?'

'If only,' she says with a sigh. We stop at the top of the staircase; Toni turns back to check that her bedroom door is still closed and Georgia can't hear us. 'I think I've got a stalker.'

THREE

Suzanne

The pool room is beautiful. It is dark outside and the place is lit with soft purple lighting. There is an awkward moment of robe removal in which everyone casts furtive glances at each other's figures, all self-conscious about their own flaws, hyper-aware of every inch of fat and each silver thread of stretch mark. Not that anyone here has much to worry about. Martha is tall and willowy, everything about her somehow fluid, nymph-like, from her flowing waves of strawberry-blonde hair to her impossibly long legs. Toni is more athletic, with strong shoulders like a swimmer's and a tiny waist. Zoe is imperfectly perfect, younger than the rest of us, unfazed by the dimples in her thighs and the barely-there rolls around her stomach that fold when she bends. Claire is shorter, slightly overweight, prettier than she probably realises and possibly the least confident among the group.

And then there is Holly: beautiful though she doesn't know it.

Just off the pool room there is a spa with steam room and sauna, with communal showers between the two. I have never stayed anywhere like this before.

'Georgia not joining us?' Martha asks, her voice thick with insincere disappointment.

'She's gone for a lie-down,' Toni explains. 'She's got a headache.'

Martha grabs a bottle of champagne, squealing like an overexcited teenager at the sound of the cork popping. She moves from person to person, filling our glasses in turn, before raising her own and saying, 'To Holly. The best friend a woman could have.'

As everyone lifts their drinks to their lips, I see the look passed between Claire and Martha. Their silent rivalry made itself known before we even got here. I wonder what the history between these two is.

'Steam room first?' Toni suggests. 'I'm freezing.'

The hot air offers a welcome warmth to my goose-pimpled skin, though I know it isn't cold alone that causes this physical reaction. Now that we are here, all together, my body feels wired, a circuit that was previously defused brought back to life. This should be wrong. It is wrong. But I needed to come here this weekend; I need to prove myself worthy of being Holly's friend, to know that I have earned my place.

'Has your dress arrived yet, Holly?' Zoe asks.

'Came last week.'

'And what a dress it is,' Martha says, moving her fingertips to her lips before kissing the air.

'Which one did you decide on? The backless one or the shorter one?'

'Backless. I should have shifted a few more pounds before now really. All this champagne's not going to help either.'

'Don't be daft,' Toni says. 'There's nothing of you.'

'I'm still not sure about it, but it's too late now.'

'What aren't you sure about?'

'The style, I suppose. Maybe I'm a bit old for it.'

'You're right, Grandma,' scoffs Martha. 'Send it back and order yourself a rain mac and a tartan skirt, and I hope you've got your blue rinse booked in for the big day.'

'You are definitely not too old for it,' Zoe says.

I find my concentration fading out as the conversation continues. No one knows Holly the way I do. They think they know her – you can see it in the way they fawn over her, raising toasts and offering compliments – but knowing someone the longest doesn't mean you know them the best. She and I have a bond like no other. A shared history, a common experience that none of the others could understand. These women – these so-called friends that she grew up with – keep things from her, secrets that must eat at their insides like acid, burning through the fabric of their guts. They have done well to keep them hidden for this long, but all secrets have a way of exposing themselves eventually.

'Are you all bridesmaids?' Zoe asks.

'Yep,' Toni says. 'Have you shown Zoe the dresses, Hol?'

'Not yet.'

Martha starts talking about the colour scheme, praising Holly's good taste and Toni's creative eye for choosing a shade and style that manages to flatter our different shapes. Thankfully I managed to get out of dress fittings with the others, having the excuse of hospital appointments. When Holly asked whether everything was okay, I told her that I've been on a waiting list for a knee operation. She has been pretty laid-back about things in the build-up to the wedding, as she is with everything, and didn't seem to mind when I asked if I could book a separate appointment with her at the bridal shop.

'I'm maid of honour,' Claire says, the comment floating randomly amid the conversation.

'Matron, you mean.'

'Sorry?'

'It's matron of honour,' Martha tells her. 'Not maid. You're married. A maid of honour is an unmarried woman. And anyway, I think you're a bit old to refer to yourself as "maid" now.'

'We're the same age, Martha.'

'*I'm* not calling myself "maid", though, am I?'

'No,' Claire says flatly. 'Because you weren't chosen.'

Beside me, and despite the steam that fills the air between us, Holly's discomfort is almost tangible. This is supposed to be a weekend for her, yet Claire and Martha are behaving like a couple of bitchy teenagers arguing over a boy at a sleepover. Holly doesn't matter to them, I realise; what matters is the competition between them, the apparent need to constantly feel that each has gained the upper hand over the other. The rest of us are just an audience to it.

These women are strangers to me, and I wondered when I was invited to this weekend why I had been kept up to now on the sidelines of Holly's life, separated like something shameful from the rest of her social circle. It smarted a little at first, though I think I understand it better now. Rather than being ashamed of me, Holly wants to keep me to herself. We have a relationship that transcends the others because we understand more about each other than they ever could. Besides, watching the way her friends are behaving makes me grateful to have been kept at a distance.

'Where's Aaron going on his stag do, Hol?' Toni asks, offering a welcome distraction from the increasingly negative mood.

'Brecon Beacons. Some sort of outdoor activity weekend.'

'In February,' Martha chips in scornfully. 'That sounds fun.'

'You know what he's like. Bit of rain doesn't put him off.'

'I don't think the Brecon Beacons is well known for its strip clubs, so that's one thing you don't have to worry about,' Claire says in an awkward attempt at humour.

'Exactly,' Martha agrees. 'You'll just need to stay on red alert for a call from mountain rescue. Where did Gareth go on *his* stag do, Claire?'

'Minehead. Seems like forever ago now.'

'Are you seeing anyone, Zoe?'

It is Martha who asks the question, though I am no longer able to see her face. I can't make out who is who now, only glistening wet flesh and the flash of different-coloured bikinis and bathing suits.

'No, not at the moment. I was with someone for a few years. We just recently split up.'

'Oh. Sorry.'

'It's all fine. What about you, Martha? Are you married?'

'God, no. Marriage isn't for me. I mean, I admire anyone who can make that sort of lifelong commitment, but forever is a long time, isn't it?'

The small, too-hot space falls silent for a moment. I thought I was fine, that I could do this, but my lungs suddenly feel as though they are filling with water, as though I'm drowning in the regurgitated oxygen of these people I don't know. My head starts to throb with the heat, a pounding at my temples reminding me that it is too late to turn back now.

'Too hot for me,' Zoe says with an awkward laugh, as though she has somehow read my thoughts, and she rises opposite me, groping for the door.

'Is she okay?' Toni asks once the door is closed behind her. 'She seemed a bit upset when you asked about whether she was seeing anyone.'

'She's been quiet all evening,' Claire says.

'You don't think she's feeling a bit left out, being the only one of us who's not a bridesmaid?' Toni asks.

'It'll be the break-up. You weren't to know, Martha,' Holly

adds, when Martha begins an apology. 'I'll go and see if she's okay.' She gets up and brushes past me as she leaves the steam room.

I wait a few moments before making my own excuses. Holly and Zoe are nowhere to be seen. I gulp a lungful of clear air, grateful for the coolness that fills my lungs. Outside the bifold doors, a swathe of night envelops the building, closing us all in. A sense of claustrophobia grips me without warning, grasping me by the throat, the breath that just a moment ago fuelled me now strangled in my chest.

Why have I come here this weekend? What am I doing? I hope this doesn't turn out to be a terrible mistake.

The surface of the pool is still, reflecting the twinkle of starlight above it. It should be serene. Beautiful. Yet it manages not to feel that way. Nothing feels or looks as it once did, the joy drained from everything with the secret I carry alone. The water glistens in the darkness, cool and inviting. It beckons to me, welcoming. At the pool's edge, I dip my toes in before climbing down the ladder and submerging myself to my shoulders.

I close my eyes as I sink beneath the surface. I wonder how long I might be able to hold my breath. I wonder how it would feel to drown. Perhaps drowning might be preferable to what I know the near future holds for me. I am already dying, and I want to scream it into the night air, have someone hear me for the first time. No one else has heard the words – not when I have not yet been prepared to admit their truth to myself.

But here they are, alive and beside me, three little words that have changed the course of everything. *I am dying.*

But I'm not yet ready to leave.

FOUR

Holly

After getting dry and putting on a pair of pyjamas, I head downstairs to the living room. Everyone else is still in their bedrooms, and for a moment I have some space to myself. I stand at the patio doors, unable to see further than a few feet ahead into the darkness of the night that lies outside the glass. I checked my phone in the bedroom, standing in different corners in search of a signal, but we are so remote out here that if it wasn't for the opulence of the barn's interior, it might feel as though we have left the twenty-first century behind. It is nice to be cut off from technology for a while, but I just wanted to text Aaron to say goodnight.

There is a noise behind me. Martha, dressed in a beautiful pair of silk pyjamas that can't possibly be warm enough for the time of year.

'Are you enjoying yourself, Mrs Henderson-to-be?' she asks, joining me at the patio doors.

'Of course. This place is incredible. Thank you.'

She shrugs off the gratitude. 'I'm just worried it's not exciting enough. I thought the others might be a bit more—' She stops abruptly, for once censoring herself.

'What?' I prompt.

She rolls her eyes. 'I don't know. Interesting, I suppose.'

'Martha.'

Sometimes with Martha it's like being twenty-two all over again. She has a need for constant excitement, for the next buzz, the next item to be ticked off her apparently endless bucket list. I understand why she is as she is, and I suppose that in so many ways she is right to live as she does, aware of how finite life is, ever conscious of time. She strives to drain each moment of every available drop of possibility. Her unrelenting energy is admirable, though it can also be exhausting.

'Sorry. I'm just annoyed by certain people's behaviour. This weekend is supposed to be about you.'

'You know I don't want a big fuss. What you've all done for me is perfect.'

'People should have left their dramas at home, though.'

'Life's life,' I say with a shrug. 'Stuff happens.'

Martha's top lip curls. 'Stop being so nice. You make the rest of us look bad.'

She glances to the living room door as though making sure no one's in the hallway. I've not heard any of the others come downstairs yet, so presume they are all still getting changed and ready for the rest of the evening.

'Suzanne seems lovely.'

'She is. After everything... she was a huge support to me. I mean, I know you were all there for me too, but she understood, you know?'

I realise what I've said, but it is too late to take the words back now. There is no one who understands loss better than Martha, and this was the very reason I couldn't speak to her in the weeks and months that followed Joseph's death. How could I talk to her about grief when the pain of her mother's and brother's deaths was still so raw?

The truth is that for a while after Joseph's death I saw little of the girls. It was partly my own doing. I shut myself away from the world, isolating Caleb and me in my bedroom at my parents' house, not wanting to face sympathetic expressions and an aftermath that I knew was inescapable. There was too much to process, and I was too immature, too naïve, to know where to start. My grief was overwhelming, and there were times when it felt my guilt would kill me. Though we talked, it was mostly through phone calls and text messages, a safe distance kept between us in which my trauma could remain abstract to them.

But it wasn't just me. Joseph had been a friend to everyone. We had all gone through secondary school together, and they were struggling to come to terms with what had happened. Everyone had lost a friend. Claire was awkward and embarrassed in the face of my grief, while Toni dealt with it in her own way, drinking too much and partying too hard. Martha's distance was immediate and obvious, a knee-jerk reaction for self-preservation after not-so-old wounds were reopened, and though I came to understand it in the years that followed, her absence felt like a kind of abandonment at the time, as though the one person who might have been able to help me – the only other one to have lost someone they loved – couldn't bring herself to be around me, my grief viral and contagious, too much a mirror of her own.

'Why was she there?' she asks.

'Where?'

'Suzanne,' she says. 'Why was she at the bereavement group?'

'Oh. Sorry. She'd—'

I am cut short by the appearance of Claire, Toni and Georgia, the latter wearing a cropped T-shirt and a pair of shorts so tiny they are little more than big knickers. Martha's reaction is immediate and unhidden, though she manages to keep her vocal response to a sigh.

'I've gone all light-headed since that sauna,' Claire says. She drops onto the sofa and pushes her fingers to her temples.

'You probably need something to eat,' I suggest. We've not had anything other than a few crisps since we got here, and I've no idea what the plan for food this evening is.

'I've got just the thing to get us started,' Toni says, and disappears to the kitchen.

'Is the spa nice then?' Georgia asks.

'Lovely,' I tell her.

'I might go and use it in a bit.'

'Great idea,' Martha says, too enthusiastically. 'You'll have the place all to yourself.'

Georgia sits at the opposite end of the sofa to Claire, curling her bare legs beneath her as though deciding to make herself comfortable in the face of Martha's obvious objection to her presence.

'Right,' Toni says, coming back into the room followed by Suzanne and Zoe. She holds out the box she got from the car earlier this afternoon when she thought she wouldn't be able to join us here. 'Who's for a snack before dinner?'

She heads straight for me, offering me first selection of the contents: an array of penis-shaped biscuits decorated with touches of white icing. 'As with everything else, blame Martha.' She pulls a face before pointing to the middle. 'That's definitely the biggest one there.'

I remove the specified biscuit. 'Martha's into baking now, is she?'

Toni raises her free hand in mock surrender. 'I was just following orders.'

Everyone takes a biscuit in turn, at once impressed and disgusted by Toni's creative use of royal icing. Martha leaves the room for a few minutes and returns with a laptop, which she opens and puts on the coffee table.

'I'll get the drinks,' Claire says. Toni follows her, offering a hand with the food, while the rest of us wait in the living room. Champagne is poured when they return, and a buffet appears as though conjured from thin air, Martha's meticulous planning and great taste treating us to a feast fit for a wedding breakfast. There is a huge platter of seafood – king prawns, clams and mussels – an antipasti selection, various canapés, warm breads and an array of fruits and vegetables.

'You could go into business together,' I tell them, taking a bite of a cranberry and goat cheese bruschetta.

'I'd eat all the supplies,' Martha says. 'I'm never sure how Toni can work at a bakery without ending up the size of a house.'

As we all settle on the huge sofas, Martha loads up her laptop. Claire smiles at me as Aaron's face fills the screen, but the expression is tinged with sadness. I wonder whether she is making comparisons, thinking back to the lead-up to her own wedding day almost ten years ago. Had she known what might follow, would she have gone through with it? The same could be asked of anyone, I suppose. None of us know what is around the corner, and in so many instances it is probably for the best.

Aaron is wearing pyjamas, his hair dishevelled as though he has been asked to film this without warning, yet he manages to look as handsome as he was on the day I met him, six years ago. He smiles awkwardly, his eyes glancing past the camera, and I realise there is someone there with him.

'Hi, Holly. You'll be at your mystery destination by now, and I hope it's every bit as incredible as it looks in the photos.'

'He's seen the place?' I ask.

'I sent him the link,' Martha explains.

'I hope you've had a couple of drinks by now, but remember

to stop at three... you've only got a month until the wedding to recover.'

'Cheeky.'

'Martha threatened to sabotage the stag do if I didn't agree to this, so it was an obvious choice really. Anyway,' and he looks past the camera again, waiting for a cue this time, 'here goes. Mr and Mrs.'

'Was there someone there with him?' I ask.

'Yes,' Martha says. 'Me. He would never have got around to it left to his own devices, would he? And let's just say that for someone with a face that photogenic, your gorgeous fiancé is surprisingly camera-shy.'

I see Suzanne's reaction to Martha's words, her shock at such an open appreciation of Aaron's looks. But this is Martha – she can get away with saying what others may not be able to. Besides, she's only speaking the truth.

'First question,' Aaron says, looking at a note in his hand. 'What is my favourite film?'

Martha pauses the laptop as Claire looks at me expectantly, eyebrow raised as she refills my glass.

'Argh. Something with Leonardo DiCaprio in it. His man crush. Um... that one where he's with Tom Hardy and they're in the wilderness somewhere.'

'*The Revenant*,' Suzanne says.

'That's the one.'

Martha presses play. '*Catch Me if You Can*,' Aaron says. 'And yours is...'

She pauses the recording again and looks to me for an answer.

'I don't know. I don't really have a favourite. Um... *Cool Runnings*.'

'What?' Toni says with a laugh. 'Really?'

'Don't judge me. It's funny. If I was having a bad day, that's what I'd choose to cheer myself up.'

Martha presses play.

'This should be easy,' Aaron says, pulling a face. 'I don't know... Holly doesn't really watch many films. Okay... something Christmassy. She loves Christmas. I'm going to go for... *Home Alone*.'

'Terrible guess,' says Claire.

'Wedding's off,' Martha jokes. 'They barely know each other.'

'I'm not reading that,' Aaron says, glancing past the camera with an expression of mock disapproval. Martha's voice can be heard whispering something inaudible. Aaron sighs and scrunches his face at what he has to say. 'Disclaimer... she made me do this.' He shakes his head before reading the question. 'Favourite sexual position.'

'Jesus,' says Toni, 'that notched up a gear quicker than expected.'

I look at Zoe, who has remained quiet since she came back downstairs. She smiles as we make eye contact, but there is an emptiness behind it, and the gesture is purely for my benefit. I feel sorry for her, guilty almost, my happiness being played out on a screen while her life has been turned upside down by a break-up. I want to reach over and flip the laptop lid down to spare her feelings, but the others have done so much to make this an enjoyable weekend that I don't want to spoil it for them.

'You are completely inappropriate, Martha Larson,' I scold.

'I know. That's why you love me.'

'Press play, please,' says Claire. 'I want to hear the answer.'

'Bloody hell,' Martha snorts. 'Someone's keen.'

I'm sure it was meant as a joke, but Martha's reaction sends a flush racing up Claire's neck. 'So do I,' I say jokingly, reaching across to tap the laptop and distract the others from Claire's embarrassment. On the screen, Aaron puts a palm to his forehead as though nursing a migraine. 'Reverse cowgirl,' he says, eyes shut, cringing.

Before she pauses it again, Martha's stifled laughter can be heard on the recording. 'Dirty boy.'

'I think that just means he doesn't want to have to look at my face.'

'No, sweetheart,' Martha says, putting a hand on my arm. 'It means you have an amazing ass.'

I laugh, but when I catch the way Suzanne looks at us, the expression on her face chases the smile from me. I am not sure whether it is aimed at Martha or at me, or perhaps it is both of us. She has only really seen one side of me, I suppose, the part of me that was drowned in grief when we met, the portion of myself that remains deadened by what happened all those years ago. Does she think this wrong, this light-heartedness? Perhaps she thinks I am being disrespectful to Joseph's memory. Either way, being under her gaze feels unsettling, as though neither of us recognises the other in this moment.

'Could I get a refill, please, Claire?' Zoe holds out her empty glass, and I am grateful for the distraction it offers. Martha resumes the recording and we work our way through a series of increasingly embarrassing questions, all of which Aaron deals with with good humour. By the time we reach the final answers, three bottles of champagne have been consumed.

'Sorry about that,' Aaron says, putting down the list of questions. 'Okay. I'm going to leave you to get on with the rest of your evening now. Before I go, I just want to say that I know I'll always be the second man in your life.'

He says something else, but I don't hear it. There is a surge in my head, a wave that crashes over every other thought, the alcohol and guilt washing all else from their path. Joseph. I see him as he was all those years ago; I hear my own words, so thoughtless, so unknowingly final. *Go then. Just leave.*

And then Caleb appears beside Aaron, awkward and self-conscious, obviously cajoled into making an appearance. He pushes a hand through his too-long hair self-consciously, nodding an acknowledgement where Martha has no doubt prompted one. I've told him that he's going to have to visit a barber before the wedding day, and he agreed, albeit reluctantly. With Dad no longer here, I have asked him to walk me down the aisle and give me away. If his discomfort on screen is anything to go by, God knows what he's going to be like in front of sixty of our friends and family.

'I wouldn't have it any other way. The woman of my dreams and the son I never wanted.' Caleb rolls his eyes before Aaron grabs him in a headlock. 'Enjoy yourselves. Don't do anything Martha tells you, okay? But seriously... have a good time. You deserve it. And I love you. Always.'

And then the screen goes black.

I smile at Martha and mouth 'thank you'. 'It was Claire's idea,' she says, in a moment of rare generosity between the two of them. 'I just carried out the threats.'

'He's surely too good to be true, isn't he?' Suzanne says. 'Good-looking, funny... Does he have a brother?'

Beside her, Zoe has gone pale. Her glass is in her hand, another serving of champagne almost drained, and I think for a moment that she might be sick. Instead, she stands, champagne slopping from her glass onto the floor as she trips over the edge of the rug, and mumbles an apology before heading unsteadily to the hallway.

'Is she okay?' Toni asks. 'She's been acting strangely since the steam room.'

'Probably the break-up,' says Claire, biting into a canapé.

I wait a while before leaving the room to follow her. If Zoe is upset, she may appreciate a little time to herself before seeing me. When I go up to her room, she is sitting on the bed. The door is ajar; she is looking at her phone. I tap gently and she drops it onto the duvet, pushing it aside when she sees me.

'You okay?'

'Yeah,' she says, forcing a smile that looks unnatural and

strained. 'I'm really sorry about what happened downstairs, Holly. I don't know what came over me.'

'You don't have to apologise. This is all bad timing for you, isn't it?'

She hesitates. 'What do you mean?'

'So soon after Dean. The last thing you need is to be watching videos like that.'

She smiles awkwardly. 'Don't be daft. It's your big weekend. I shouldn't have reacted like I did. I've probably had too much to drink.'

'You didn't seem to eat very much. Shall I bring something up for you?'

She shakes her head. 'No, thanks though. Maybe you're right. I'll come back down in a bit.'

I turn to leave.

'Holly.'

'Yeah.'

'Please don't feel sorry for me,' she says, her eyes watery. 'I don't deserve it.'

I say nothing, waiting for her to continue. Her face looks pinched, as though she's suppressing something she wants to say. 'Things with Dean... It didn't end the way I told you. It was me. It was my fault.' She looks down, thumbing the hem of her pyjama top. 'I didn't tell you because I didn't want you to think badly of me. But it is bad. I deserve to be judged.' She looks back up, barely meeting my eye. 'There was someone else.'

FIVE

Claire

In the living room, Martha, Suzanne and I sit on the sofas, having fallen into a silence that manages to feel oppressive. We have discussed the barn, Holly's forthcoming wedding and our jobs, and now that the conversation topics have dried up, I feel inexplicably like the outsider, as though Suzanne in particular would prefer me not to be here. I'm not sure why I feel this way, or what it is about her, but I wish Toni was still here to offer a diversion. She disappeared not long after Holly went to see Zoe upstairs, presumably going to check on Georgia.

After telling me on the landing that she thought she had a stalker, Toni fell into a reluctance that I couldn't persuade her out of. She refused to say anything more about her suspicions, dismissing them as paranoia and a result of insufficient sleep. Now, thinking about her words and about the way she looked when she told me – drawn and exhausted, something real in the fear that crossed her face – I think she believes it's true, despite her attempts at denial. I will try to speak to her again later, or perhaps tomorrow, when it's just the two of us.

I reach to the coffee table for the open bottle of champagne. 'Top-up?'

They both nod and I fill their glasses before reaching for my own. I have already had enough, but it is not yet 9.30, and it would be a waste of a rare child-free weekend if I was to call it quits so early on the first night.

'We all owe you money, Martha,' I say. 'For the robes.'

'You don't owe me anything.'

'You should have mentioned that you were going to order them.'

'They're a gift. If I'd wanted money for them, I would have mentioned them.'

There is yet another awkward moment of silence. 'It was very kind of you to order them,' Suzanne says, and it feels as though she is trying to undermine me, to make my objections look silly in order to ingratiate herself with Martha for some reason.

'I wonder whether we'll see Toni again this evening,' Martha muses.

'She must have been very worried about Georgia if she wasn't prepared to leave her for the weekend,' Suzanne says. 'Do you think she thinks Georgia might hurt herself?'

'I don't think so.' I want to put an end to this conversation before it has time to develop. It already feels like cheap gossip, and it wouldn't be fair on Toni for us to sit here discussing her business. Hypocrisy stabs at my insides, and I slug a mouthful of champagne in an attempt to drown it before it can settle in for the evening.

'She might for the attention,' Martha says, glancing sidelong at me and raising an eyebrow. I know what she's referring to. A few summers back, Georgia went missing. She was fourteen at the time and was gone long enough for local media to grab hold of the story. She was found almost twenty-four hours later, hiding in a derelict house with a boy she was at school with, the pair claiming not to have realised that anyone would be looking for them. I can't imagine how worried Toni must have been during the entire day and night she was missing, and Georgia's comment to the police must have felt like a slap in the face to the woman who has done everything for her.

'She's always been impulsive, hasn't she?' Martha adds.

'It's a difficult age,' Suzanne says diplomatically.

'They fight more like sisters than mother and daughter.'

I cast Martha a glare, willing her to stop talking or to at least change the subject, but if she notices the hint, she chooses to ignore it.

'We all argue with our mothers,' Suzanne says.

We fall into silence. Suzanne obviously doesn't know Martha's history, and I wonder now how much Holly has told her about us all. None of us have met her before; she lives outside of Bristol, somewhere near Gloucester, I think, and by all accounts leads a relatively quiet life. I get the impression from what Holly has said previously that social occasions aren't really her thing.

'Georgia's got Toni under her thumb,' Martha says, breaking the silence. 'She always has done, ever since she was a toddler. She was manipulative at the age of three... Do you remember that time she cut her own hair and then told her mother that Caleb did it?'

'Children can't be manipulative at three years old,' I tell her.

She raises an eyebrow cynically. 'If you say so. You're the expert, after all.'

'How old are your children?' Suzanne asks, the question a welcome distraction from Martha's increasingly argumentative tone.

'Seven, five and four.'

'Wow,' Suzanne says. 'You're a busy lady then.'

'I wouldn't have it any other way,' I say, feeling a disconcerting need to defend myself. I know what Martha thinks of the boys, that they are undisciplined and spoilt. The latter might be true – aren't all children spoiled these days? – but she has no idea how difficult parenting is, and she has based her judgements on rare and brief meetings with the children, never really taking the time to talk to any of them or get to know them. Our lives are so different in so many ways that perhaps we will never be able to get on as we once did, back when we were still just teenagers.

Martha turns her head towards the patio doors, though it is so dark outside that nothing can be seen through them. I know where she has gone; where she always goes when she falls into this kind of absent silence. It is why I can never hate her, despite how often it may seem she tries to push me towards it. She is just as messed up as the rest of us, but the shine she's able to apply to her life makes it easier for her to hide the fact.

'Holly told me you're in property development, Martha,' Suzanne says. 'How long have you been doing that?'

My mind drifts quickly, their voices fading as I grow distracted. Realising I have been excluded from the conversation, I get up and go to the kitchen. The champagne has warmed me, bringing a flush to my face, and when I open the bifold doors, a welcome blast of cold night air whips through the room. There was a time when I was younger when I used to smoke, using it as a desperate attempt to fit in at parties, finding the smokers more sociable than the non-smokers. Now, I wish I had kept up the habit, for nothing more than something to occupy me while my mind turns over the conversation I've just left.

At times, I have wondered whether Martha hates me. Sometimes I wonder how the four of us have remained friends for all these years. It has been almost two decades since we left school, and in that time our lives have changed beyond recognition. We have become different people, and yet in so many ways perhaps we are not that different at all. Holly was always the clever one, Toni was the wild child, Martha was the free spirit, and I was... What was I? I was just there, I suppose. Dependable. Safe. Boring. When I look back, it is obvious that Martha and I were only ever close because Holly tethered us, the invisible glue that kept our friendship group together. Would I have remained in contact with Toni if it hadn't been for Holly? Perhaps not... I don't know.

With the thought of Toni comes her voice. I hear her distantly at first, little more than a whisper, before realising that she is closer than she sounds. I go to the light switch and submerge the kitchen back into darkness. Her voice drifts on the night air, then I hear another. Georgia. They are near the outbuilding, where the spa is.

'You have... me,' I hear, the sentence broken, her words lost to the night. 'I can't... to help... don't.'

In the darkness, I grope my way around the worktop, navigating the island and the dining table before finding the door to the corridor that connects the two buildings. I open it slowly, not knowing where Toni and Georgia are, and not wanting them to hear me. When I inch through the gap, I see that the door at the other end is open. There is light spilling into the corridor, the gentle glow of the pool room's soft lighting. When the voices come again, they are louder now, the corridor echoing the sound.

'You've never listened.'

'That's not true. I might not have always understood, but I've always listened.'

'You don't hear me, though, do you?' Georgia snaps.

I should stop listening now. I should go back into the kitchen and pretend I was never here; allow them this time and space to dissipate whatever friction sits between them without the presence of an unseen audience. Instead, I stand with my back to the wall of the corridor, listening as their conversation plays out.

'It's just come as a shock, that's all.'

'Why?'

'What do you mean?' Toni's voice is thin with tiredness, as though this conversation has already been had.

'Why has it come as a shock?' Georgia challenges, anger rising with every word.

'I didn't even know you'd been seeing anyone.'

I have heard too much. I know too much. My life is already consumed with more problems than I am able to juggle alone; selfishly, I don't need to be in receipt of anyone else's dramas. I want to walk back into the house and return to Martha and Suzanne, erase what I have heard. But I have stayed out here. I have chosen to listen.

'But you weren't seeing anyone either, were you? That's not necessarily how it works, is it, Mother?'

Martha is right about one thing: Georgia can be awful. Her words are cutting and cruel, designed to slice a wound into her mother's flesh. The moment's silence that follows is evidence that they have achieved the desired effect. Then there is movement; a door being opened. A rush of cold air swirls around my legs, cutting through me with a bite. Toni calls after Georgia, says something, but the words are too distant now to make out.

I go into the pool room, where the bifold doors are open. Toni and Georgia are in the garden, neither dressed appropriately for the freezing cold, and their voices must surely be carrying to the main building now.

I wait in the shadows, watching as Toni grabs her daughter by the bare arm. 'You can't bury your head and pretend it isn't happening. Don't make the same mistake I did.'

'Mistake?'

'Georgia,' Toni says, her voice instantly weakened, desperate. 'I didn't mean it like that. Georgia, please.'

But Georgia has already shoved her mother's hand from her arm and is hurrying from her, running now across the lawn, fleeing into a night that is heavy and suffocating. Toni follows; she is fast, but not as quick as her daughter. I watch as they fade into the darkness of the garden, heading for the gates that lead to the lane. There are no street lights for miles, nothing to illuminate the blanketed darkness; nowhere for them to run to. Georgia is impulsive and reckless; there is no knowing what she will do, or what she is capable of.

'Toni! Toni!'

If she hears me, Toni ignores my calls. I run after them, each step pressing the damp of the grass through my socks. It is so dark that by the time I reach the gates, neither Toni nor Georgia is anywhere to be seen, though I still hear Toni calling her daughter, telling her to stop, reminding her that there's nowhere to go. I call after her, but her name sounds small in the vacuum of the night air, the word whipped away by the wind.

The lane is narrow and dark. Trees hang overhead, forming an arch that cuts off the light of the moon, shrouding me in a cocoon. I feel suddenly claustrophobic, despite the breeze that chops at my limbs and the tunnel of road that stretches ahead of me.

It is too quiet. Other than the noise of the wind in the branches above, there is nothing, as though Toni and Georgia have disappeared. I am out here alone. I stop and stand in the middle of the lane, a sudden fear creeping through me with a quickly increasing intensity. It is unnaturally dark, the hedgerow and the trees merely shadows against the blackened sky. There is barely a sound, yet I become acutely aware of the ringing in my ears, a crescendo that rises to become unbearable, just me and it alone out here.

But then the ringing in my head is severed by something else. The sound is low at first, remote and detached, but as it nears, I realise it is getting too close too quickly. I move to the side of the lane and press myself against the hedgerow, head turned to one side as the car's lights illuminate the trees ahead. The driver is going too fast. He must know these roads.

Joseph appears in front of me, a memory so vivid that it feels as though he is here, his face exactly as it was the last time I saw him that night. His expression is blank, emotionless, and I have to close my eyes to free myself of the sight of him. Darkness engulfs me, the noise of the car's engine surging as it approaches. This was him, I think. The night he died. Alone in the dark, the wrong place at the wrong time.

I open my eyes; the headlights blind me. I don't see the driver, unable to make out anything but the burning brightness, but I hear the squeal of the tyres on tarmac as the car veers away from me, missing me by just inches. My heart judders in my chest as I fall back against the sharp hedgerow, my knee twisted and face scratched as I lose my footing. Heart pounding now, lungs fighting for breath, I try to right myself, but I find myself stuck, rooted between the present and the past, guilt fixing me to the spot.

The car might so easily have hit me, and if it had, it would have been some kind of karma for what happened all those years ago.

SIX

Suzanne

It is 10.30, and half the group has gone AWOL, the alcohol proving more than some are apparently able to manage. I assume that Toni is somewhere with her daughter, and Zoe hasn't been seen downstairs since her disappearance following Aaron's video. Claire must also have gone up to bed, leaving Holly, Martha and me sitting by the fire. I can't imagine that Martha will head upstairs before we do. I get the impression that she likes to be the life and soul of the party, the last woman standing. She doesn't want to miss out on anything, though we are all so champagne-tired by now that I doubt there would be much to miss out on.

I hope my assumptions about her are right, and that she stays here with us.

'I feel a bit guilty,' Holly says, throwing a glance to the living room door.

'About what?'

'Whatever's happened with Georgia. Toni missing out.'

'She hasn't missed out,' Martha says. 'She's here.'

'She's not herself, though, is she? She seems on edge.'

'Does anyone know yet what's happened?' I ask.

'Probably something trivial,' Martha says with a flick of a hand. 'Georgia's eighteen. Boyfriend's dumped her or something.'

Martha can be tactless sometimes, and I am able to say this without knowing her. We all know Holly well enough to know the details of her past. At eighteen she fell pregnant and gave birth, and in that same year she lost her partner and became a single parent. These things were far from trivial. She endured more during her teenage years than many people have to experience in a lifetime.

Though I think she must acknowledge Martha's insensitivity, Holly gives it no attention. 'Why wouldn't Toni just tell us that, though?' she muses.

Martha shrugs and sips her champagne. She has a high tolerance for alcohol: between the six of us we must have had seven bottles, and I've only drunk two glasses. It barely seems to have touched Martha, though.

'You know what Georgia's like,' Martha says, as though this alone explains everything.

I know why Holly tolerates Martha's abrasiveness. I imagine that much of what she says and does is overlooked because of her past, as though losing her mother and brother in such terrible circumstances provided a future free pass to abandon the mental filter that might once have regulated what crossed her lips. Holly has sometimes spoken about Martha's past, though never in any great detail. I know that she was only thirteen when the fire happened. Her mother saved her, managing to get her out into the garden before going back into the house for her brother. Neither of them was seen again.

The survivor's guilt must have felt at times impossible for Martha to bear.

'I don't know,' Holly says dreamily, lost in her train of thought. 'Something doesn't seem right.'

'All you need to focus on,' Martha says, leaning forward to pick up her glass, 'is enjoying this weekend. Everyone else's problems will have to wait.'

And yet it already seems that they can't. Toni and Georgia have brought whatever secret the two of them now share, and it is clear that Zoe's break-up is hanging over her like a bad omen. I have brought my own problems here too, though I have kept them to myself, for now. We are none of us without our issues. Some people are just able to hide them better than others.

I wonder what Martha would make of my life if I were to share the details of it. She has wealth and beauty, yet I know that behind the hardened veneer there is something softer, a vulnerability that she prefers to keep hidden. She wants people to regard her as capable. She wants to be seen as a leader, as someone to be admired and respected. She would think my life sad, with its confinements and its limitations. I have been to few places; I have seen few things. My existence is small and contained, shaped by routine and structure. I am safe when there is a pattern to things. Spontaneity scares me, and there's something about Martha that's unpredictable and, I suspect, volatile.

I feel myself growing too hot beneath my blouse, so I excuse myself and go to the spa, where I open the doors and stand out on the lawn, breathing in the crisp night air. There is no sound, and for the first time I consider that I may never have heard true silence before. Even in the most remote of places, there's always some sort of background noise – distant traffic, some furtive scuttling of wildlife – but here there is nothing, and I am unsure whether it is a comfort or a threat.

I reach into the pocket of my robe and take out the box of

cigarettes and lighter I put there earlier. My mother always hated the habit, though it sometimes felt as though she hated pretty much everything about me. Either that, or the things she did like she just decided to keep to herself. Once, after one of her particularly bad episodes, I smoked in the garden right below her bedroom, letting the scent of tobacco rise like steam to her open window. She was bedbound at the time, not long home from one of her many hospital stays, unable to react with anything but words.

But I paid for it, in time, when she recovered.

I am pulled from my thoughts by a sound behind me. Martha is at the door to the corridor that links the spa with the house. In the darkness she's little more than a silhouette, framed in the doorway like a ghost. 'Did you want to be alone?' she asks. 'I just wondered if you're okay. I hope I didn't upset you earlier?'

'How would you have upset me?'

'All that talk about Toni and Georgia,' she says, waving a hand dismissively. 'Sorry. A total bore for anyone who doesn't know them.'

The irony doesn't pass me by. Just how well does she really know Toni? I doubt she knows about her secret online activities and what she does to make extra money; no one seems to know about that, not even Georgia.

'It's fine,' I say, blowing a lungful of smoke away from her.

I feel her watching me, her focus on my face sending a flare of heat through my chest. 'Have we met before?' she asks.

'I've been told I've got one of those faces.'

'I thought maybe Holly had made a mistake when she said we'd never met. You seem familiar, that's all.'

'Want one?'

She flinches when I hold out the packet to her, and then I remember why it prompts such a reaction. The fire that killed her mother and brother, started by an abandoned cigarette.

'I don't smoke. Thanks.'

The truth is, I know far more about Holly's friends than she realises. As close as Holly and I are, she wouldn't understand it; she would think it strange that I have sought out so much information about the people she chooses to spend her time with, which I suppose in some ways it might be. But when you want to get to know someone – to really get to know them – you need to find out all the details of their life: their interests, their ambitions, the people they choose to call their friends. It seems to me that Holly has surrounded herself with people who need her, though from what I've seen so far, I don't think she needs any of them.

'Holly okay?' I ask.

'She's decided to call it a night. We're the last women standing.'

'I'm quite proud of that,' I tell her. 'I'm usually in bed by ten.'

She laughs. 'I'll let you in on a secret – me too. Just don't tell the others; they seem to think I'm some sort of socialite.'

'Your life does seem pretty glamorous, by all accounts.'

Martha rolls her eyes. 'Yep,' she drawls. 'Put enough filter on anything and it can look impressive. Smoke and mirrors.'

She falls silent at her own words, and I wonder whether her mind has returned her to that night and to the fire. I have read reports about it; I have gleaned as much information from Holly as she has been willing to impart. She is a loyal friend, not prone to gossip, and as such, what I know has been left mostly for me to find out. It didn't take long to discover that the public's opinion of Martha's father turned decidedly sour after the fire. There have been hateful things written about him online, the success of his business deemed undeserving; trolls questioning whether he should be allowed responsibility for housing others when he couldn't even keep his own family safe, despite the fact that no charges were ever brought against him. Throughout it all, Martha has remained loyal to him, yet I wonder whether that might have come at a cost.

'I love your hair colour,' she says.

'Thanks.' I put a hand to the silver pixie cut that last summer replaced the mousy-brown non-style I'd had for forever. 'I call it my midlife-crisis look.'

She laughs. 'It really suits you. I've always wanted to be able to pull off short hair.'

We fall into a silence that seems to last a moment longer than is comfortable.

'What do you do?' she asks, drawing me back from my musings.

'Sorry?'

'For work. What job do you do?'

'Oh. I work in a library.'

'Nice. Do you enjoy it?'

'I love it. I love books, I love being on my own, I love the peace and quiet. Except for Tuesdays and Thursdays, when the baby sing groups are on,' I add with a smile. 'Thankfully, they're short.'

'You're a woman after my own heart. I don't know how Claire does it, to be honest. Screaming kids all day and then home to three of her own. No thank you.'

She watches me as I drop my cigarette stub to the ground and stand on it. 'I'll clean up in the morning,' I tell her.

'Don't worry, I won't grass you up.'

She is standing close, so close that I can smell her perfume. The make-up that was perfect when we arrived here this afternoon has been softened by the steam of the spa room earlier, a smudge of foundation gathered at her jawline. I feel an urge to touch it, to rub her skin until it is smooth again. Perfect.

Her perfection seems to highlight my every flaw, and I am suddenly self-conscious beside her, too aware of the contrasts between us. Martha is vibrant and alive, while I stand beside her slowly dying, everything I once was and might have been now sucked from my body by the parasite that lives within me. I want to tell her; the words feel lodged in my chest, pressing against my heart as though they might pierce it. But I haven't even told Holly, and Martha is little more than a stranger to me.

She is so close I could reach out and touch her. And just like the silence, I am unsure whether her closeness is a comfort or a threat.

SEVEN

Claire

When I return to the barn, Toni is already back. She's sitting alone at the dining table, in the darkness, eating a dry slice of sourdough bread. Her skin is so pale it looks almost translucent, ghost-like, and I can smell the cold that clings to our clothes.

She fiddles with an earring distractedly. 'How much did you hear?'

'I saw the light on in the pool room,' I tell her. 'I went to see who was there.'

She raises her head and pushes a lock of bottle-blonde hair from her face. 'That's not what I asked.'

'I heard you shouting Georgia's name.'

She looks at me, the tiny ring in her nose flashing a spark in the darkness, but it is hard to make out her expression. Perhaps she believes me. Maybe she doesn't.

'You don't like my daughter, do you?' Her words slur slightly, the champagne making them slippery on her tongue.

'None of you do.' I hear her breathing change, a sharp intake of breath as she tries to pull herself together. For the second time today, I think she might cry. Please don't do it here, I think. Not now.

'Where did I go wrong with her, Claire?'

'Don't say that. You haven't done anything wrong.'

'She's not a nice girl, though, is she? Don't,' she says, raising a hand, apparently able to read a reaction I thought I'd suppressed. 'I'm her mother, so I'm allowed to say what everyone else thinks. The truth is, I'm not even sure that I like her.' She takes another bite of bread and sighs. 'What did you hear outside, Claire?'

I sit opposite her at the dining table. I can't lie to her again, not when she clearly knows that I heard far more than I admitted to. 'Is she pregnant?'

'History repeats itself,' Toni says flatly. 'And why wouldn't it?'

'What do you mean?'

Toni shrugs. 'I'm a fuck-up, Claire. All she's ever seen is me moving aimlessly from one brief relationship to another, so what have I taught her?'

'That's not true,' I respond, though it would be fair to say that Toni has never had much luck with men, partly because she always seems to be attracted to the wrong ones. There have been plenty of casual relationships along the years, many with men she has never introduced to her friends, but most of those we did meet all managed to raise red flags before our drinks were finished. 'You've taught her about hard work and determination, haven't you? You set up a business on your own, without help from anyone, and you did it as a single mum. Not many people can say that.'

Toni looks back at the wedge of bread in her hand, studying it as though hoping to find some sort of answer to parenting in the curve of its crust. 'Do you know what she said to me once?

She said that whoever her father was, he made the right choice
not to hang about. She said that wherever he was, she wished
she was there with him.'

She reaches for a half-finished glass of champagne and looks
at me for longer than is comfortable. I'm unsure whether she is
waiting for me to say something or whether she's simply
studying me for a reaction, trying to gauge my views without me
having to give them a voice.

'And the worst bit,' she adds, 'is that for a split second, I
wished the same.'

She drains the glass before setting it back on the table.

'Teenagers say horrible things to their parents,' I offer,
trying to appease her. 'God, the things I used to say to my
mother at times. I didn't mean any of them. Neither does
Georgia.'

'There must have been some truth there somewhere,
though,' she challenges. 'At times, at least.'

We sit in silence, lost in our separate thoughts, before being
thrown into light when someone flicks the switch at the kitchen
doorway. Holly gasps when she sees us, obviously not expecting
to find anyone sitting here. 'God,' she says, putting a hand to her
chest. 'You almost gave me a heart attack.' She looks from Toni
to me and then back again. 'Is everything okay?'

Now the light is on, I can see the mascara smudged beneath
Toni's eyes. Her face looks gaunt, the deep lines at the corners
of her mouth too prominent; she has lost too much weight when
there was already little there to lose. The smell of salmon
catches me from the remains of the seafood platter left at the
other side of the table, making my stomach churn with nausea.

'All fine,' Toni says, with a forced smile. 'Just, you
know... waste not, want not.' She gestures to the remaining food.
'Want anything?'

'No thanks.'

She stands, embarrassed now at having her emotions on

display beneath the beam of the kitchen spotlight. She runs a finger beneath each eye in turn, trying to get rid of the evidence of her tears. 'It's later than I realised. You don't mind if I call it a night, do you, Hol?'

'Of course not. I think most of us already have. I won't be long – I just came to get a glass of water.'

'Ever the sensible one.' Toni puts a hand on her arm as she leaves. 'See you in the morning.'

'What's happened?' Holly asks me once we've listened to Toni go upstairs.

'Georgia. She's okay, they just had a bit of a row. Anyway, are you all right? Are you enjoying yourself?'

'Of course I am. Really,' she adds, when I raise an eyebrow. 'Did you manage to get hold of Gareth?'

'No signal. I'm sure they're all fine. Pizza, film, late night... they probably didn't notice I wasn't there.'

'I'm sure that's not true.' She sits beside me at the table. 'I know you don't want to talk about it this weekend, but when we get back, maybe you two should go to see someone.'

'A counsellor, you mean?'

'Maybe. If that's what you need. I could get some names from work for you if you like – it would all be completely confidential.'

The truth of Gareth's gambling and the mess he had got us into came spilling out a month ago, at the surgery. I had gone in for a routine smear test, but as soon as I saw Holly I couldn't hide the fact that something else was wrong. By then, I had already known about Gareth's habit for over a year. She took me into an empty treatment room and sat me down, and before I could stop myself, I'd told her everything. It felt good to be free of it all for a couple of moments, as though in offloading it onto someone else I was detoxing myself. It was a feeling that didn't last long enough.

Holly means well, but talking to a stranger won't make any

difference. There's not a counsellor in the world who could save Gareth and me now, not after what he's done. Not after what I've done.

'I don't know. I'm not sure I want it. I don't want to be around him at the moment, Hol. He's put us all through so much. The kids are too young to know what's going on, but they've sensed the change in mood, you know? How am I going to tell them that we have to leave our home?'

Holly's face creases with concern. 'It hasn't come to that, has it?'

'Not yet, but we're not far off.'

I drink some more champagne, a deep hiccup heaving at my chest. I hardly ever drink any more. I am always with my children, always driving one of them to swimming lessons or football training, forever cooking something or cleaning something, fixing scrapes and toys and tears. If there's ever a moment when they're not with me, I'm either working or doing something for them – prepping lunches, ironing uniforms; booking trips or ordering new trainers because someone has gone up another shoe size. Being needed has grounded me in so many senses, and I love the fact that I am the centre of these little humans' worlds. It gives me a sense of purpose and pride. I just wonder sometimes how it feels to be me. Just me. I hoped that this weekend might offer a glimpse of the person I once was, but I think it's too late to find her now. She's gone.

'There's always a way around things,' Holly says optimistically, though I've told her enough for her to know that this may no longer apply to us. Things are worse than I have admitted to her. Gareth didn't confess to his gambling habit until it was already an addiction, and only then under duress, when he realised I knew too much for a lie to persuade me otherwise. I had begun to suspect something weeks earlier, though I had tried to ignore the warning signs. Then I checked our savings account – something I hardly ever did. Why would I? I had a husband I trusted, someone who worked as hard as I did to secure our family's future.

By the time I accessed the account, Gareth had ripped through our combined savings, the accumulation of years of hard work and sacrifice. He'd gambled with our future, with our children's futures, and now it might cost us our home.

'I've made such a mess of everything, Holly,' I blurt, the words tripping over a sob. 'I haven't handled anything like I should have.'

'Claire,' she says, taking me gently by the shoulders. 'This is not your fault, okay? Maybe I'm speaking out of turn here, but it's all Gareth's doing. He's got you into this mess – he's the one who needs to get you out.'

If only he could, I think. If only he would try. There have been so many arguments after the boys have gone to bed, so many angry and bitter exchanges in which the most awful things have been said. I have threatened divorce. I have told him I wish I'd never married him. In return, he has tried to blame me for his failings, suggesting that my need to control everything has pushed him away, driving him to find a satisfaction elsewhere that he no longer gets from me, when all this time I have been trying to help him, still willing to bail him out if I can only find a way to.

But for the past week before coming here, I couldn't bring myself to look at him. His deceit, my deceit. Where do we go from here?

I shake my head, tears falling freely. 'He can't. Not this time.'

'What do you mean?'

I take a deep breath and push the heels of my hands across my eyes, wiping away my tears. This is selfish and ill-timed; my problems are not for here, and they are certainly not for Holly. She is my closest friend, yet there are things I could never tell her. Things I can never admit I have done.

'I'm sorry. Forget this conversation ever happened, okay. Please?' I raise my glass and force a smile. 'Cheers.'

'You don't have to—'

'To the hen weekend,' I say, cutting her short and forcing an enthusiasm that she knows is strained.

She tilts her head and sighs. 'To the hen weekend,' she says, clinking her glass against mine. 'Thank you for all this.'

'I've barely done a thing. I haven't had a chance to... Martha did everything.'

I try not to say it with bitterness, but it is difficult. In so many ways, Martha's desire to be the organiser has made life easier for me, taking away the pressure of having to make sure this weekend is the one Holly deserves. The hen party arrived at the worst of times really. I have been unable to focus much on anything other than our dire financial situation and the mess it has made of our marriage, and so it was right, I suppose, for Martha to take over.

'I think I've upset her,' Holly says.

'How?'

'The whole maid-of-honour thing. I wasn't choosing one friend over another; it wasn't like that.'

'No one thinks that.'

'I think Martha might.'

Embarrassingly, I feel my eyes start to fill again. 'Perhaps you should have asked her instead,' I say. 'I don't deserve it. I shouldn't even be a bridesmaid.' I mean this more than she could ever imagine.

'Listen to me,' she says, putting a hand on my arm. 'You're an amazing friend. We all know it. Even Martha. And you are a brilliant mother to your boys and an incredibly loyal wife. Lots of women in your position might have just walked away and let their husband deal with the mess he's made. Stop giving yourself such a hard time.'

Tell her. Tell her.

But I can't bring myself to do it.

'Martha hates me.'

'Why would you think that?'

'Come on, Holly. You've seen what she's like. She's always making snide remarks – it's like we're still at school.'

Holly sighs. 'She doesn't hate you. She's jealous of you.'

'Jealous? What is there to be jealous of?'

'Your family. Your relationship.'

I raise an eyebrow and laugh scornfully. 'Yeah. Great, isn't it? She's really missing out. She can have him if she wants him.'

Holly pulls a face, chiding me for being flippant. 'Okay, things aren't perfect at the moment, but you've got stability. Or at least you did have,' she adds, putting a hand on mine. 'And you'll find a way to get it back.'

I should tell her. I should tell her here and now, while we are alone and I have the opportunity. All the secrets. All the lies. I should have told her at the time and spared her so much, but it's too late now, it's too late, it's too late.

'I'll snap out of this, I promise. I'm sorry.'

'You've nothing to be sorry about,' she tells me. 'We probably all need to go to bed.' She stands to go to the sink for the glass of water she came in here for. 'I don't know how I'm going to do this all again tomorrow.'

We go upstairs together, and when I get to the bedroom, Zoe is in the single bed at the far side of the room. Her back is to me, so I have no idea whether she's asleep or not, but if she hears me come in, she doesn't make a sound. I find my phone and use its light as I quietly search through my suitcase. The conversation I had with Holly just now replays in my head, details ebbing and flowing, a tide bringing them to me before dragging them away again. She is so kind. So thoughtful.

If only she knew, I think. If only she knew what was really happening to me. My heart starts to thud in my chest when I can't find the envelope I brought with me, clothes thrown from

left to right. I thought I had tucked it into the inside compart-
ment, pushed right down to keep it hidden, but it is no longer
there. I feel sick at the thought that someone might have seen it.
That someone has taken it.

And then I find it, concealed among a pile of underwear, its
white corner peeping between folds of black cotton. My heart
shudders and slows, a long sigh of relief escaping me. But it
doesn't last long. As I open the envelope, everything is brought
back.

It is the last of the letters, typed like all the others: short,
succinct, damning.

> I need more. Another 5K and I will leave you alone. Find it, or
> I will tell Holly your secret.

NOW

SUNDAY

Outside, another few inches of snow has fallen. She said this would happen. No one listened to her. No one wanted to listen. This weather was forecast, wasn't it? Or was it? She can't remember now. She doesn't seem able to recall much before these past five minutes, and those are moments she wishes she could forget. Her past life is over, she realises it in the here and now: there is a divide between what she came here with this weekend and what now faces her, a future stretching into seemingly endless darkness, impossible and unknown. Perhaps that will be the case for all of them; that all their lives as they knew them will be obliterated by what has happened here.

'Have you called an ambulance?'

'Of course I've called an ambulance. I called them ages ago, but they're not going to get here, are they? We're in the middle of fucking nowhere in two feet of fucking snow!'

'Don't go in there!'

But it is too late; she is in the water. There is screaming, the worst sound she has ever heard: a low, guttural moaning like a mortally wounded animal. The blood in the pool disperses as the water is disturbed, the puddle of crimson that had risen to the surface fading into a mass of pale pink. She flails, the body weighed down by wet clothing, the submerged face petrified, nightmarish, as her head is turned to the purple glow above.

The screams. They fill her head with such an all-consuming completeness that she believes she will never be free of the sound; that it is the only thing she will hear from now until forever. She needs to run somewhere, to hide, to escape this place, but there is nowhere to go.

'You!' someone screams. 'This was you!'

The sobbing is broken, an awful silence settling over each of them, freezing them in the moment. She can't look up; she doesn't know how to begin to face what she has done. She can't look up, but she has no choice.

'What did you do to her?'

She looks up. The faces that greet her are anguished and accusing, each one a reflection of the horror that has settled inside her, where she fears it will remain forever. Everything has been destroyed this weekend. None of them will ever be the same again.

TWENTY-SEVEN HOURS EARLIER

EIGHT

Holly

I go to Martha's bedroom before going to my own, wanting to thank her for all the effort she has put into this weekend. When I get there, she is sitting in the chair at the side of the bed, so lost in another world somewhere that she doesn't notice me standing at the doorway. Alone, she looks different to the Martha we have seen downstairs this evening. She appears small and vulnerable, something child-like about the way she sits with her legs tucked beneath her, her slim limbs wiry, their corners sharp. She looks frail in a way I have never seen her.

'Martha.'

A hand flies to her chest as she turns to me.

'Sorry. I didn't mean to make you jump.'

'I was miles away. Come in.' She moves her legs from beneath her, leans to the bed and taps the duvet, welcoming me to join her.

'I just wanted to say thank you,' I tell her, closing the door behind me.

'You've done that already. And you really don't need to. I'm sorry things haven't been better.'

She is still disappointed in how the day has gone, though I was hoping to reassure her that she needn't be. It has been good just to spend time with everyone, and I need little more than that. Martha strives for perfection, knowing really that such a thing doesn't exist but the pursuit of a possibility offering her eternal optimism. There have been so many times when I have envied her that. Without hope, what else is left?

'Suzanne seems nice.'

'She is. I think she was pleased to be invited this weekend. I don't think she does very much.'

'What makes you think that?'

'I'm not sure. Just her lifestyle, I suppose. She keeps herself to herself.'

Martha tilts her head, looks at me and smiles. 'She's lucky to have you. We all are.'

'I think I'm the lucky one.'

She smiles again before her face falls, seriousness pulling at her features. 'Tell me again how you met her.'

'Suzanne? At the bereavement group.'

I know that Martha already knows this; she can be many things, but she is not forgetful. We have talked about the bereavement group on more than one occasion, Martha usually the person to bring the subject up. I think she has wondered in the past whether something similar might have been useful to her, though pride would always have kept her from sharing her innermost thoughts with a room full of strangers. She has rarely spoken to any of us about what happened that night, and I have always suspected that the memories of it are stronger than she allows us to believe. She needs to be seen as someone in control, and though she has never said it, I suspect that she regards any kind of group therapy or counselling as a sign of weakness.

'What's the matter?' I ask.

She shakes her head. 'Nothing. Perhaps I'm being silly.'

'But?'

She pulls her long legs up, folding them beneath her again. 'Who had she lost?'

I smile sadly. 'Lost,' I repeat. 'It's a funny way of putting it really, isn't it? Well, you know, not funny. It kind of suggests someone's been a bit careless, like misplacing a set of keys. "I've lost Joseph... does anyone know where I put him?"'

Martha reaches for my hand and clutches it in hers. 'You have to stop doing this to yourself. It's been almost two decades. You deserve to be happy.'

I wipe my eyes with the sleeve of my robe. Perhaps she is right. The more time that has passed, the easier it has become to believe that the platitude is right. Time and distance seem to have fooled me, allowing me to build a protective cocoon. If I tell myself the same thing enough times, eventually I may start to believe it's the truth.

'And what about you?' I ask her. 'Have you taken your own advice?'

She smiles sadly. 'You know I am very much a "do as I say not as I do" kind of person.'

'What I said to him that night—'

'Holly, everyone argues. Everyone. It wasn't your fault. You could have said anything to him at that party and the outcome would have been the same – you couldn't have stopped what happened. You were not responsible for it.'

I sigh and pull away from her. 'Do you ever think what life would be like now if, you know...' I don't need to say anything more; she knows what I am talking about. Who I am talking about.

'All the time.' She puts a hand on mine and holds my gaze,

fierce in her defiance, resolute that no vulnerability will be reflected from her eyes. 'Aaron is a good man. He makes you happy. You don't need to think about anything else.' She pulls her hand away and sighs. 'You still haven't answered my question about Suzanne.'

'What question?'

'Who had she lost? Why was she at that bereavement group?'

'Her mother died. Why do you ask?'

'She said something earlier. I didn't think much of it at the time, but later it didn't make sense.'

'Who said something? Suzanne?'

Martha nods. 'She said, "We all argue with our mothers."'

'She's got a point,' I say, trying to make light of the comment, though in truth I can't remember the last time my mother and I had a cross word. Perhaps I am lucky in that sense; maybe our relationship is not the norm.

'It doesn't seem strange to you?'

'Strange in what way?'

'It doesn't strike me as a normal thing for someone who's lost their mother to say. I wouldn't say that.'

She's looking too deeply into this, but I can't tell her that. Martha is sensitive to the subject, and she doesn't know Suzanne in the way that I do; she isn't familiar with her phrasing. They're just words, I think. They're just words.

She seems to sense my doubt. 'It was like she was talking about her in the present tense.'

Her words send a chill snaking through me, though I know it is ridiculous that they should do so. I am tired. I've drunk too much champagne. Everything appears distorted when viewed through a fog of alcohol and sleeplessness.

This time it is my turn to take her hand in mine. 'Thank you for today.'

'You're ignoring what I just said.'

'I'm not ignoring it, I just...'

'You just think I've lost the plot.'

I pull a face. 'It's been a long day. We've all had a lot to drink.'

Her eyes widen. If it wasn't my hen weekend, I'm pretty certain she might now accuse me of being patronising. She is censoring herself out of respect for the occasion, whether or not I am deserving of her doing so.

'I'm sorry. Come here.' I open my arms to her, and she hugs me, though it feels reluctant. 'Have a good sleep.'

'You too. You need to recharge for round two tomorrow.'

'You are relentless, Martha,' I tell her, getting up from the bed.

'I know,' she replies with a smile. 'You wouldn't have me any other way.'

I go back to my own room, expecting Suzanne to be in bed already. She isn't here. I don't know where she might have gone. Perhaps she's chatting with one of the others in their bedroom, or maybe she went outside for another cigarette. Either way, it leaves me with little time before she returns.

Martha's words prey on my mind, despite my attempt to explain away Suzanne's comment as an unusual choice of phrasing. I consider the possibility that Martha misheard what she said, or misinterpreted it in some way, but even after alcohol, Martha is meticulous. I have known her to bring up details of conversations we had months earlier: she has the kind of memory that we all envied back at school, able to retain information and pass exams with seemingly minimal effort, nailing barely-revised-for A grades while the rest of us pulled teeth to scrape our passes. She is so particular about things that she rarely makes a mistake.

But I know too that the alcohol is making me paranoid. I can't remember the last time I drank so much – probably not since my twenties, when I was still young and foolish enough to not consider the raging headache and carpet tongue that would follow – and I know my body isn't going to be happy with me in the morning. Suzanne's mum died three months before we met. Our friendship was built on the shared experience of grief. She has been a source of comfort to me on so many occasions during the past eighteen years, always available at the end of the phone on the days when it felt as though the world might close in above my head and crush me.

So why am I wasting so much thought on something I know is irrelevant?

It's the drink, I tell myself. It's just the drink.

But still Martha's words stay with me, taunting me with their persistence.

It was like she was talking about her in the present tense.

Suzanne's phone is on the bedside table, plugged into its charger.

It isn't something I have ever done before, nor is it something I even want to do, but if I can access her phone, I may be able to dismiss Martha's suspicions within moments. It will put my own mind at rest, though I know rationally that there is no reason for it to be unsettled.

Don't be stupid, Holly, I reprimand myself. This isn't you.

But apparently it is.

I go to the bedside table and pick up the phone. It is locked with a four-digit PIN, but if Suzanne is anything like I am, it shouldn't be too difficult to work out. I try the year: 2022. It doesn't work. I try 1234, hoping for impossible predictability. I try the year she was born: 1983. The screen lights up; I am in. I guessed it might be easy, but I never thought it would be as straightforward as that. But what is my own PIN? The year of Caleb's birth. Not exactly difficult for anyone to work out, if they were inclined to do so.

A photograph greets me on the home screen: Suzanne sitting on a low wall at a seafront somewhere, a pebble beach stretching out behind her. She is smiling for the camera, though it seems more that she is smiling at whoever is on the other side of it, the unseen person whose finger captured the image. I wonder who she was with. In all the years I have known her, she has made few mentions of any partners. She seems to live a quiet, simple life, content with her job, her home and her cat; she makes jokes about herself as a spinster, happy with her status. There have been times over the years when one or both of us has been busy, when our friendship has seen quieter periods, as all friendships do when adult life gets in the way. But we have always come back to one another at some point, bound by our respective losses, tethered by the mutual experience of grief and bereavement.

My fingers quiver as they move across the screen, guilt shaking in their tips as I access the contacts list. This is stupid. I trust Suzanne.

I trust Martha.

I freeze at a sound on the landing, but there is nothing to follow it. I know I should take this as a warning, that I should put the phone back and end this madness, yet something propels me onwards, and I do neither.

I scroll hurriedly through the alphabetic list of names, my fingertips speeding across the Fs and Gs. I reach M, and my heart stops in my chest, a single word severing everything I thought I knew.

Mum.

NINE

Suzanne

I am at the bifold doors in the kitchen, the last woman standing. Here, with this desolate winter scene stretching out in front of me, I could almost believe myself the final woman left on earth. Despite Martha's attempts to stay awake, she almost fell asleep on the sofa beside me, and when I gave her a shake to rouse her, she mumbled something about Holly before heading upstairs. I am grateful to be here alone, free to enjoy another cigarette in peace.

'Sleep tight, Mum,' I whisper to the night air, raising the cigarette aloft as though toasting her with a glass of champagne.

I take a long drag before blowing a thin trail of smoke into the darkness. When I was younger, she hated the fact that I smoked; hated the fact that despite her reprimanding me for the habit, I continued to keep it up. Being a disappointment seemed to come as second nature to me, whether I tried to make it that way or not.

It is snowing. The coal-black night is flecked with tiny shards of falling silver, and when I turn off the kitchen light, I am rewarded with my own private theatre, the sleeping world playing out on the wide stage of the doors as I stand here, its only audience. The moon acts as a spotlight, casting an eerie glow over the lawn; the woods, too far to see in the darkness, are hidden behind the backdrop of the night. A thin layer of snow dusts the patio area like icing on a cake. Confetti at a wedding.

I never appreciated the world around me enough before the diagnosis. People don't, do they? We are all so busy going places, meeting deadlines, we miss a lot of the here and now, all the peaceful moments that pass unnoticed because we fail to spend enough time just *being*. But a diagnosis changes that. I've started to see things around me that I never realised until recently were there. I see the minutiae of people and of circumstances when so much was lost to me before.

I see things I know others fail to see.

From the corner of my eye I notice a movement, something so slight it might have been easily missed. I scan the garden, adjusting to the darkness, and then the creature moves beneath the light of the moon, stalking to centre stage, a nervous first-night performance. I have never seen a fox this close up before. Its movements are slow and graceful, and when it stops, it is just metres from the doors. Its head turns and it looks right at me, our gazes meeting, both of us frozen. The tiny white pinpricks of its eyes flash as it continues to stare, waiting for me to be the first to break focus. I feel transported to a different country, a different world – somewhere wild and unpopulated. How nice that might be, I think, to live in a place where there are no people, just creatures like this beautiful animal, silent and unobtrusive.

My daydream is disturbed by a sound, and I turn my head towards it. My focus is broken; the fox wins the game. Music, quiet and distant, is sunken into the air, carrying weight in the darkness. I thought myself alone, but I am not. When I put the kitchen lights back on, the fox is gone. The music is still here, a dull beat, but when I go out into the hallway, it fades and is lost. The rest of the house is asleep and silent. I return to the kitchen and open the door to the corridor that leads to the spa. Music floats down the passage, a heavy, repetitive bass accompanied by inaudible lyrics. I stand still in the darkness, training my ears to the sound. It is rap music. Young. Inaudible lyrics. It can only be Georgia.

At the end of the corridor, I stop before the doorway. The pool is at the far end of the room and the lights above the water have been turned on, tiny stars sparkling – an artificial night sky beneath the real one that sleeps outside. From where I stand, I am able to see her stretched out on one of the loungers lined along the side of the pool. Her tanned skin glistens wet, patches of flesh illuminated by a light that rises and dips in the shadows of the barely lit room.

I crouch to the ground, steadying myself where I can watch without being seen. Then I realise that Georgia is naked, her clothes discarded on the tiles. A light comes from her phone, casting a glow across her body. She arches her back, pushes out her breasts, pouts for the camera. I feel a heat rise in me, embarrassed at the indignity she is exposing herself to. I want to go and cover her up, to ask her what she thinks she's doing, to talk some sense into her, but she is nothing to do with me.

She holds the phone out in front of her, assessing an image, then her thumbs move erratically as she taps something out on the screen. There is a curse beneath her breath before she throws the phone onto the lounger next to her and gets up. As she turns, our eyes meet in the darkness.

I fall back into the corridor, unsure whether the noise I make as I stumble is loud enough to be heard. But it surely must be. She is just at the other end of the room, and the darkness carries sound in the way feathers are carried by a breeze. She will know that someone was watching her. But she won't know it was you, I try to reason with myself. Yet I can't allow myself to be persuaded. She looked right at me. She saw me.

I hurry along the corridor back to the house. If Georgia wants to pursue me she has time to catch up with me, yet she doesn't, and when I get back through the kitchen I stop in the hallway by the front door and allow my body to unfurl itself from the coil it has been wound into. I wish I could go home; I wish I'd brought my own car here so that I could collect my things now and leave.

I need to go to bed. I mustn't sleep, not now, but I need to think. What do I do now? What have I done?

Upstairs, I linger at the door to the bedroom I'm sharing with Holly. I don't go in. Instead, I go to Martha's room, waiting with an ear pressed to the door to see whether I hear movement. When I don't, I gently push down on the handle, easing the door open. The room is dark and smells of her perfume. The light from the landing casts a triangle across her sleeping body beneath the duvet, her head turned to one side on the pillow. I go into the room, easing the door shut behind me in case anyone should walk past, leaving sufficient light for me to see the contours of her sleeping face. She has removed the make-up she wore earlier, her skin pale and shiny with night cream. Her hair curls in a twist at the nape of her neck, somehow perfect even while she sleeps.

There was a moment earlier, just before Martha and I came back inside from the garden, when I thought she might ask me something else. There was a brief moment when her eyes met mine for just a second too long, but for whatever reason, she changed her mind. I wonder what she was going to say. I wonder whether there was something she wanted to know about me. Whether there was something she wanted to tell me about herself.

I sit at the side of her bed, in the oversized armchair on which she has draped the dress she wore this afternoon. The fabric is expensive, soft against my skin. I have never worn anything as beautiful as this, and I wonder how it would feel, how it would make me feel – whether in wearing something so different, I could morph into another person somehow. Another version of myself.

Martha stirs beneath the duvet and my body tenses. I have no excuse prepared, no plausible reason for being here in her room while she sleeps. I wait a beat and her breathing steadies itself as she falls into a deeper rest, her eyelids fluttering slightly. Then I lift the fabric gently between my fingers and edge my way around the bed, taking the dress to the free-standing mirror at the other side of the room.

I take off my oversized cardigan, pull my pyjama top over my head and wriggle free of the matching trousers. My naked reflection is shadowed by the night, but I am able to see enough for the differences between my figure and Martha's to be high-lighted. Where her frame is long and willowy, mine is curved and soft. Where her hips are narrow, mine are rounded. I think the dress won't fit me, yet when I try it on, it does. The fabric is pulled tight at my hip bones and around my chest, but I could be anyone, anywhere. Perhaps the lack of light is assisting the transition, helping to fade me out.

Still in her dress, I return to Martha's bedside, to the chair next to where she sleeps. Her chest rises and falls gently, every-thing about her as perfect as it was before. She is a pale goddess from an old oil painting, her beauty captured and preserved in time. I have an urge to touch her, to rouse her from her sleep. I want to wake her, to tell her that I forgive her.

There are so many things I want to say to her, words I

expected myself to have said by now. I came here this weekend for Holly, but more than that, I came here for Martha; yet above all else that has happened today, one thing has made itself obvious: Martha doesn't remember me. She might have thought she recognised me, but she has no idea who I am.

TEN

Holly

On Saturday morning, with nagging temples that berate me for drinking so much champagne last night, I find everyone else already in the kitchen. Claire is preparing scrambled eggs, the smell sending my stomach into turmoil, while Martha pours coffee, busying herself with playing the host despite the amount of alcohol she consumed last night. Even Georgia is here, though she doesn't interact with anyone, sitting on one of the dining chairs with her legs pulled to her chest and scrolling through her phone beneath the table. Suzanne is at the sink, her back turned to the room, and I am grateful for not having to make eye contact with her yet, as though she might see what I did last night reflected there.

I heard her come to the bedroom not long after I'd accessed her phone, so I quickly returned it to the charger, then got into bed and turned out the light so that when she came in I could pretend to be asleep. She may not have believed the act, but she made no effort to speak to me. It took me an age to find sleep, too distracted by the incessant repetition of Martha's words and by the contact I had found on Suzanne's phone. *Mum.* The word wouldn't leave me, the possible 'what ifs?' keeping me awake, desperate for an explanation. Her mother died almost two decades ago. What if there is someone else she refers to as 'Mum'? What if she still owns her childhood home, the house number stored as it would have been all those years ago?

'Good morning, sleepyhead,' Martha greets me, waving a teaspoon in the air like a magician about to perform an elaborate illusion. 'Coffee?'

'A gallon, please.' I sit beside Toni and allow my head to loll onto her shoulder. Her blonde hair is damp and darkened, pulled up into a messy knot at the top of her head. 'Have you all showered already?'

'I went for a swim,' she says, 'so I had one at the spa.'

I sit up when Martha puts a coffee in front of me. 'Get that down you and then brace yourself for round two,' she instructs me with a wink.

'Oh God.'

Zoe sits across from us, pushing a piece of toast around her plate. This morning, now sober, I wonder whether she regrets last night's confession. As soon as the words left her, she seemed to wish she could retract them, immediately changing the subject, repeatedly apologising for bringing her problems with her on the trip. Perhaps she is worried that my opinion of her will be changed by her admission. I'm trying not to judge her for it, though it has surprised me. Spending most of our days sitting side by side at the reception desk at the surgery means we have chatted on and off about all manner of subjects, gaining countless details of each other's lives. I always got the impression that she was completely loved up with Dean, that they would marry and start a family together, but I suppose no one ever knows what is really going on behind closed doors. And no one ever really knows what is going on in someone else's head.

'Finally,' Georgia says, to no one in particular. 'Wi-Fi's working.'

'Are we still going to the pub for lunch?' Toni asks.

'I'm up for it.'

'Me too.'

'We should walk,' I suggest.

'Really?' Martha glances at the bifold doors, gesturing to the fine layer of snow that frosts the patio and lawn.

'Don't tell me you've only brought heels with you?'

'In light of your suggestion... my answer is now yes.'

'I've got a pair of wellies in the boot you can borrow,' offers Toni.

'Wellies?' Martha eyes her as though she has spoken a foreign language. 'Why do you keep a pair of wellies in your car?'

'Come on,' I coax her. 'It'll be good to get some exercise and fresh air. We can walk off the alcohol ready to start again later.' I throw her one of my persuasive smiles, a look I know she is unable to resist.

'Are you okay, Zoe?' asks Claire.

When I glance at Zoe, her face has paled. Her eyes look dark and sunken, and I suspect it wasn't just yesterday's alcohol consumption that kept her from sleep last night. She nods, but the hand that moves to her stomach speaks a different response. 'I'm okay,' she says. 'I just feel a bit sick, that's all. Sorry. All that champagne.'

She gets up and runs to the downstairs toilet. Martha waits a few moments before rolling her eyes. 'Is she trialling as a magician's assistant or something? These disappearing acts are becoming a regular feature.'

Toni laughs, but something in my reaction makes her stop

and she busies herself with taking used mugs and plates to the sink.

'If the Wi-Fi's up and running now,' I say, 'I'll go and check what time the pub opens.'

I go upstairs, but I don't make it to my bedroom. The door to Claire's room is open, someone inside. I see a flash of clothing, a pink hoodie. Georgia is in there. I didn't notice her leave the kitchen. I watch as she moves items on the dressing table, searching among them for something. Then she goes to the side of one of the beds, where she reaches for a suitcase.

'What are you doing?'

She turns sharply, knocking her thigh against the bed frame. 'Holly,' she says innocently, a syrupy smile stamped on her face. 'I didn't hear you.'

Obviously not, I think. 'What are you doing in here, Georgia?'

'I've lost an earring. This room is so gorgeous, isn't it? I mean, the whole place is amazing.'

Despite how sneaky Georgia is capable of being, she is also a terrible liar.

'Lose them both in here, did you?'

She smiles awkwardly as she puts a hand to her hair, pulling her fingers through it distractedly. 'What?'

I point. 'No earring in either ear. You must have lost the other one as well.'

Her hand moves to her ear, continuing the charade. 'Oh. Well... I lost it last night.'

'It's probably in your own room, don't you think?'

'Probably,' she says. She moves past me, making a point of turning side-on. She is trying to hide something from me, something hidden in her hand, but I don't catch sight of what it is.

I look at Claire's suitcase, wondering what is in there to have caused so much interest. I scan the contents briefly, feeling guilty at doing so. Make-up bag, dresses, underwear... nothing out of the ordinary. So what was Georgia doing?

I sit on the edge of the bed and scan the room. There is a toiletry bag on the dressing table, left half zipped, embroidered with Claire's initials. I go to it, peep inside; see the bottle of pills that is tucked between the tube of foundation and a travel-sized hairspray. Xanax.

'God, Claire,' I mutter to myself.

I wonder how she got the tablets; they aren't available on the NHS. More to the point, why has she been taking them? Claire has always been a nervous person, and I know she's suffered from depression in the past, but that was all years ago now, long before she had the boys. I know that her anxiety has made a return in recent months, but she attributed most of the pressure she's been under to having three young children to look after. Until Gareth's revelation, that is. Now I imagine he is the cause of most of her stress.

I turn the bottle in my hand. This is his doing. This is Gareth, not the boys. But Claire is usually against the idea of any mood-enhancing medication. Years ago, when her depression was at its worst, I remember how she shunned the suggestion of antidepressants, too scared by the possibility that she would develop a dependence on them. Even at her lowest, she wouldn't take something she regarded as a potential risk. I turn the bottle of Xanax in my hand again. It doesn't make sense. The pills contradict everything I know of Claire, which makes me wonder just how bad things have really become.

I sit in the chair by the dressing table, my mind distracted for a moment from Claire, thoughts of Suzanne once again taking centre stage. Though I don't want to have to listen to it any more, I can't silence the voice that keeps telling me something is wrong. That she has lied to me. But why would she have done that? I have gone back over what happened last night so many times, each time stalling on the look that Martha gave me, so certain of the words she spoke. *Mum.* Nothing makes sense.

I return the bottle of Xanax to Claire's toiletry bag, pushing it the bottom where it will be hidden among the other contents. Then I go to my own bedroom, heading straight to where Suzanne's phone was last night, plugged into its charger. It is no longer there. I search through her things before finding it tucked beneath her pillow. Did she hide it there on purpose? Does she know what I did last night? But she can't do; I am being paranoid again.

I unlock the phone. If she knew, she would have changed her password, but it remains the same. As I did last night, I access her contacts list. Suzanne lives by herself, or so she has told me, yet it occurs to me now that I have never been to her house. She has never invited me. Why?

With shaking hands and the memory of Martha's words still ringing in my ears, I press the green call button. I allow it to ring for longer than I should do. There is no one there to answer it. Of course there's not; there's been a mistake somehow.

And then there is a click. A voice. A woman voice's, weak but curt. 'Hello?'

There is a silence that feels impossibly long, though in truth it must last mere moments. I feel my heart pound painfully in my chest, so loud that I'm sure the woman must be able to hear it at the other end of the line.

And then I finally bring myself to speak the word. 'Mum,' I say, my voice barely there, kept nondescript so that she might be fooled into thinking she is speaking to Suzanne. And it works.

'Suzanne?' she snaps, her frail voice managing to be fuelled with frustration. 'Is that you? When are you coming home?'

I end the call, cutting Suzanne's mother dead.

ELEVEN

Claire

I woke too early this morning, my body clock rousing me at the time my sons would usually come crashing into the bedroom, waking me with a tangle of limbs and a flurry of demands, all cuddles and kicks. The bed felt cold; I missed the heat of them beneath the duvet with me, their skinny arms wrapped around me. I wondered how they'd slept, and whether they had missed me too.

I feel caught in an uncomfortable kind of limbo this morning, not feeling up to the day ahead but not wanting to be back at home either. I have longed for some time away from my life for so long, a little respite from the noise and the chaos that comes with a house full of boys, but now that I'm here, it doesn't feel like I thought it would. I shouldn't have drunk so much champagne last night. And I wish I'd never overheard that conversation between Georgia and Toni.

I watch Toni now, washing dishes at the sink, and I wonder

how she is managing to keep their secret to herself. Georgia's pregnancy... fears of a stalker. She is a bag of nerves, so loosely held together that she should jangle when she walks, yet she manages to keep going, existing behind an almost perfectly maintained facade, as I suppose we all do. Something jabs at my side, some invisible stab of guilt. We all have secrets we want to keep from each other, and some are worse than others. I know that all too well.

'The snow's come to nothing,' Martha says. 'Every year we get the same: "Britain Faces Worst Winter in Forty Years".' She lowers her voice in an exaggerated newsreader style and rolls her eyes as she mocks my concerns over yesterday's forecast.

'Give it time,' Suzanne says.

Holly returns to the kitchen. 'Zoe's going to catch us up,' she explains.

'Shall one of us wait for her?' I suggest. 'We shouldn't let her walk to the pub alone, should we?'

'I have offered, but she insisted she'll be okay. I made her promise she'll call when she leaves.'

Thoughts of how the boys are doing this morning continue to distract me. I check my phone for a message or a missed call from Gareth, but there is still no signal anywhere to be found in the house. Even if communication between us was possible, I wonder whether he would want to talk to me. He has been giving me the silent treatment for a while now, pouting and sulking like a fourth child, somehow managing to make me believe that our financial problems are my doing. It's the guilt, I suppose. In making me culpable, he must in some way be able to escape his own responsibility.

Despite Martha's protestations, we manage the walk to the pub. I need the fresh air and the exercise, and I'm grateful to be alone for a while, escaping the inane chatter of the rest of the group. We reach the point at which the car almost hit me last night, and a chill passes through me at the memory, something pulled back from the darkest recesses of my brain.

I finally manage to get a signal once we're near the pub. I try Gareth's mobile, but there's no answer. When I call the house phone, it rings through to the answer machine.

The pub is one of those modern gastro places that serves decent home cooking at fancy restaurant prices, every ingredient artfully arranged on the plate in an attempt to fool customers into thinking that they're getting something worthy of the bill. Everyone orders soft drinks, giving our livers and our stomachs a chance at some sort of recovery before Martha inevitably breezes us all into another champagne-supping session once we're back at the barn. For now, the mood is quiet and subdued, though she does her best to instil enthusiasm among the less energetic of us.

As I'm finishing my meal, my phone screen lights up on the table beside me, Gareth finally returning my call. I go outside to speak to him, as much for the privacy as for the signal.

'Everything all right?' I ask.

'Seb's had an accident.'

'What? What's the matter with him?'

'He's fine now, there was just... He had a fall.'

'What sort of fall? What's happened?'

I hear him sigh. The audible equivalent of an accusation, the implication that whatever has happened is somehow my fault.

'He was at the top of the slide and—'

'In the garden?'

'Yes,' he snaps.

'Is he hurt?'

'Just a couple of scrapes. He's fine.'

'Was he up there on his own? Why weren't you watching him?'

'I've got three of them to watch – I can't have eyes everywhere.'

And yet I'm expected to, I think, managing to keep the response to myself for now. I'm expected to work, to pay half the bills, to do most of the housework – all while making sure that our three children are fed and clothed and safe and happy. That they're not falling from the top of slides while I'm distracted by something else apparently more important.

But this is how it is. This is how it has always been. And it's my fault; I realise that now, too late. My fault for just accepting it.

'Where were you?' I ask.

There is silence. I imagine him in his makeshift office beneath the stairs, scanning betting sites while the boys run amok, oblivious to anything beyond his own selfish impulses.

'I was helping Alfie with his homework.'

He is lying. I have known him for long enough to know when he's telling a lie, although recently it feels that everything he says is soaked in some kind of half-truth. Not being able to trust my husband is a sad fact that has taken me a while to come to terms with, but here I am, prepared to accept it now that it has become unavoidable. I can't trust him with our finances. I can't trust him with our children. I am married to a liar.

Perhaps I got what I deserve.

'What did he have?'

'What do you mean?'

'Alfie,' I say, trying to keep my voice calm. 'What homework did he have?'

The pause is too long, an empty space in which his mind has time to process a succession of possible responses before landing on one that seems the best fit in the moment.

'Just some maths stuff,' he replies.

The problem with lies, even the smallest ones, is that once they're told, they create a chain. If I was to ask him for details now, innocuous, seemingly pointless specifics about what this 'stuff' involved, then he would need to remember it all for future reference, in case the subject was to arise again. But lies are hard to hold onto – slippery, malignant things that are difficult to keep under control. It is only the truth that stays in place, solid and unchangeable. No one needs to deliberate over the truth or worry about being able to remember it.

The irony of my own thoughts makes me cringe. The truth is that recently I have been more than a little forgetful, the line between fact and fiction not always as distinct as I know it should be. I misplace things, forgetting where I've put them. Sometimes forgetting what I was doing with them in the first place. I recall conversations differently to the person I shared them with, details confused and specifics neglected. It's the Xanax, I know, and yet now that I've started, I can't stop. They take the edge off my anxiety, if only for a short time. They make everything easier, and I need that, no matter how briefly.

I snap my focus back to the here and now, resenting the silence that sits between Gareth and me. I know that Alfie's homework for next week is to design a football kit; I saw it on the class app on Thursday evening. It doesn't need to be done until the end of the week, so I was planning to help him with it after school on Monday. Gareth doesn't have a clue; I don't think he ever downloaded the app, and I doubt whether he even knows what topic they've been studying for the past few weeks.

'Seb's okay then?' I ask, refusing to be drawn towards an argument, not while I'm away and supposed to be enjoying myself.

'He's fine. Just missing his mum.'

And there it is – the stab of emotional blackmail that manages to make me feel guilty for being myself for a couple of days, the knife tip aimed directly where he knew it would hurt the most. In Gareth's mind, Seb's fall is probably my fault. I should be there, at home, with the kids. I'm not supposed to ever take a break or have any time for myself; that's not how this parenting thing works, is it? Not for me, at least. I barely get time to order myself new clothing online when I need it, let alone browse gambling sites for the best opportunity available to lose a family's life savings.

'Well, give them all a hug from me,' I say, refusing to rise to the bait. 'I've got to go – the others are waiting for me.'

There's no 'Love you' or 'Have a nice time' before he hangs up – just a 'Bye then' and a click as he ends the call. It shouldn't be like this, I think. I shouldn't be made to feel guilty about enjoying myself or for leaving the boys with their dad for a couple of days. They are his children too. He is as much a parent as I am. It's easy for him. Easier than it is for me, anyway.

I don't want to resent my husband, but I do. I don't want to hate him, but sometimes it feels as though we have almost reached that point, and once we're there, where do we go then?

I am distracted from my self-pity by the sight of a car further along the lane. It has pulled over at a passing point, its engine still running. I recognise the number plate. I noticed it yesterday as I waited at the front of the house, registering the combination of letters. *BLD*. Like blood, I remember thinking. I want so much to believe that I am wrong, that I have made a mistake, but I know there is no error, no coincidence.

I press myself against the hedgerow, visions of last night's near-accident returning to me like snapshots of a nightmare. I watch as Zoe gets out of the car before leaning back in through the door to say something to the driver. I wait for him to pull away, a few more seconds in which to convince myself that I am mistaken somehow. But I am not. The same car was parked on Holly's driveway yesterday morning. It is Aaron's.

TWELVE

Suzanne

It starts to snow again before we get back to the barn. The sky is unusually grey and overcast, the air dense in the way it only manages to be when it precedes snowfall. I imagine that in heavy snow the barn must be cut off from the nearest villages. We would find ourselves stranded here, though no one else seems particularly concerned by the prospect.

Martha's itinerary states that when we return from the pub we will use the spa before doing some cocktail-making, so this is what we do, everyone heading to their bedrooms to get themselves ready. Holly and I go up to our room together. At lunch she sat at the other end of the table, Martha separating us, and on the way back she walked behind us, lagging with Toni, so there has been little opportunity for us to talk to one another yet today. Now, she barely acknowledges me as we get changed, only speaking to ask if I have seen her hairbrush. I have done something to upset her, but I don't know what.

When we get to the spa, the mood is decidedly different to that of yesterday. There has been a shift this afternoon, some unspoken friction cutting a web of division among the group. Toni seems to be somewhere else, tired and distracted, and Claire is a bag of nerves, constantly checking her phone. Even Holly seems changed in some way, keeping a distance that has become more obvious as the day has gone on. The more I consider what I may have done to upset her, the more paranoid I become about it.

Unable to bear the heat of the sauna, I sit alone by the pool-side and dip my toes into the water, grateful for the chill it sends through my limbs. All sense of time seemed to slow a while ago, these past few months a blur of hours and days that have merged into one, though this weekend it seems to have come to a stop. I could be anyone, I think. Anywhere, in any time.

I am not alone for long; Toni comes to join me, casting off her robe by a lounger and sitting beside me. She is wearing a black swimsuit, her strong shoulders glistening with teardrops of water that slide down her bare skin. She says nothing to me, yet in the silence I get the impression that there is plenty she would like to say, and that she would appreciate someone to talk to.

'Penny for your thoughts,' she says. 'Where does that expression come from, I wonder?'

'No idea. And I don't think mine would even be worth that.' I nod to the sauna. 'Not enjoying?'

'Headache.'

'Is Georgia okay?' She didn't come down to the spa with us, choosing instead to stay in the living room and watch television. She has been with us so little in the twenty-four hours since we arrived here that I wonder what the point in her coming was. Surely she is capable of looking after herself for a couple of days? And whatever problem was causing her such distress yesterday, she seems to have made a full and quick recovery from it.

Toni just nods, giving nothing away. 'Do you have kids?'

'No.'

'Wise move,' she mutters, looking at the surface of the water. There is a moment of silence, more awkward for her than it is for me in the echo of her words. 'That was a joke, obviously. A bad one.'

'I imagine they can be hard work once they hit a certain age.'

Toni rests back on her hands and tilts her head to the ceiling, lifting her face to an invisible sun, perhaps imagining – or wishing – that we were somewhere else: a white-sand Caribbean beach, perhaps, or a heat-soaked square in a European capital. Had travel been easier, or had Holly's wedding been booked a few years earlier, we might have done either of these things, but she seemed happy to stay in the UK, insistent that she didn't want too much of a fuss.

Outside, it is still snowing, the ground now layered in a fresh dusting of white, the bare branches of the trees at the far edge of the lawn a frozen scene stolen from a Christmas card.

'You're making the cake for the wedding then?' I ask, guessing she might be keen to change the subject from her daughter.

'Yep. It's my gift to Holly.'

'Lovely. What are you planning?'

'I'm doing a three-tier blush-pink and gold floral design, ruffles on the bottom tier and flowers on the top. Holly and I designed it together.'

'Sounds beautiful. I had a look at your website when Holly mentioned you to me – your work is amazing.'

'Thank you.'

In truth, I didn't stop at Toni's website. From there, I moved to newspaper and magazine articles about her award nominations; I read reviews left by customers and scanned her social media pages for things I could learn about her; things that would help me feel less of an outsider. One particular theme recurred among the praise heaped on her, two words seemingly used more often than any others. Single mum. There was much admiration of her determination and drive when setting up her business, starting with cake-baking in her parents' kitchen to renting her first bakery at the age of just twenty-four, all while caring for her young daughter. The praise is deserved.

And yet I wonder what she makes of the focus on her motherhood, the fact that no matter what she achieves, her successes are always underpinned by her status as a mother, everything else coming second to this fact. Every accolade is accompanied by a comment on her teenage pregnancy, with the unwritten suggestion that it must have been somehow more difficult for her, or that she has something more to prove. She isn't a successful businesswoman, she is successful single mother, everything else an add-on to this first and most prominent achievement.

And then there are the other things I found. The things that her friends here this weekend probably know nothing about. A series of images flit through my brain, inappropriate and provocative. I glance to the sunbed on which Georgia lay last night, naked and pouting for the string of selfies she snapped. Like mother, like daughter.

'You've all known Holly since high school then?' I ask her.

'Primary. The four of us went right through school together. Seems a lifetime ago now. Where did you go to school?'

I hesitate on an answer, teetering between the truth and a lie. In the end, I opt for the lie. 'Cheltenham,' I tell her, hoping she won't be too familiar with the area.

She sighs and sits upright. 'It's not true, is it, what they tell kids about school being the best days of their lives. Mostly it's just a series of disasters and counting down terms until you're old enough to escape the place. Bit like prison, I suppose, just without the crime. Did you enjoy school?'

'No.'

'I fucking hated it.'

'You didn't have the best of experiences, though, did you?'

Her head snaps towards me, her expression questioning and edged with defensiveness. She has misinterpreted my words, misunderstanding what I was referring to. She thinks I am talking about Georgia. 'What do you mean?'

'Joseph. Losing a friend like that... it must have been so difficult for all of you.'

The tautness in her features stays fixed in place. 'Yeah,' she says. 'It was difficult for everyone.' She looks past me. 'You must know a bit about him then, you and Holly meeting in the way you did?'

'Yes, she's told me things. She was really in love with him, wasn't she, despite being so young.'

Toni looks across the pool, the surface of the water reflecting in her shining eyes. 'Yeah. She was.'

'Did you all know him then? Everyone here this weekend? Holly talked a lot about him when we met.'

'Not Zoe. Holly's only known her since Zoe started working at the surgery a few years back. But the rest of us went to school with him.'

I want to ask her more, but it is difficult to do so without it seeming inappropriate, which of course it is. It's a shame. There is so much I want to know.

'I'm going to get a drink,' I say. 'Do you want anything?'

Toni rejects the offer. When I get to the kitchen, Georgia is there, sitting at the dining table and scrolling her phone. 'Do you want a hand?' she offers, watching me go to the cupboard for glasses. The offer is so unexpected and so seemingly uncharacteristic that for a moment I am suspicious of it, contemplating an ulterior motive. There is something about the girl that is untrustworthy, and it seems to me that a person doesn't need to know her to be able to see it.

'Thanks. I was going to take them through to the spa.'

Georgia goes to the fridge and takes out a bottle of champagne. 'This, I'm guessing?' She gives the bottle a wave before opening it, impressively adept with a cork for someone of her young age. I balance a tray of champagne flutes and she follows me along the corridor. Zoe has joined Toni by the side of the pool, and within moments the others appear from the sauna, Claire red-faced and sweating.

'You read my mind,' Martha says, eyeing the champagne bottle and offering me an appreciative smile.

I pour a glass for everyone. Some are more reluctant than others, still suffering the after-effects of yesterday's indulgences.

After everyone has taken a sip, they return to the water and the poolside. Some take their drinks with them, others leaving them on the table while they swim. I carry mine to one of the loungers and sit down, lying back and taking a moment to try to think about nothing. For the past couple of months I have developed an array of distraction techniques, training my mind in the art of diversion. At times I have found myself impressed by my brain's ability to remove itself from the inevitable, but there are other times, such as now, when it seems almost impossible to tear myself from the only thought I know it will always come back to.

This weekend, there have been plenty of things to keep me distracted. Other people's problems have taken the place of my own, allowing me to find some respite from my trauma. It is while I am lying here, trying to deter my mind from a return to home, that I notice Georgia has returned to the table. No one else seems to pay her any attention, everyone engrossed in conversation or swimming, but as I watch, she turns her back to the pool, as if to hide whatever she is up to from the rest of the room.

I get up and go over to her. 'What are you doing?'

There is something in her hand, something that she conceals from me. I want to grab her by the arm and prise her fingers open, but I'm reluctant to make a scene in front of everyone else.

I look at the drinks, trying to remember where everyone left them before getting in the pool. When I turn to look around, Martha is drinking from her glass. I can't see any of the others'.

'Is that Holly's?' I gesture to the glass on the end, the one I'm certain Georgia's focus was on. I lower my voice, the words leaving me in a hiss. 'Were you about to spike her drink with something?'

For a brief moment, Georgia looks panicked, her heavily made-up eyes darting to the door as she searches for an escape route. 'No,' she says, though there has been too long a hesitation. 'Don't be stupid.'

'You sure I'm the stupid one?'

She opens her mouth to respond, then, remembering her mother is just behind us in the water, thinks better of it. I reach for her fingers and force them open, and she allows me to do so without objection, knowing that just one word from me will expose whatever little game she was about to play. My earlier doubts about her and the thoughts I had towards her in the kitchen not long ago are confirmed: Georgia is dangerous. There is something venomous about this girl, something that runs far deeper than just her angst-ridden teenage years.

'Shall we ask your mother?' I suggest, turning to the pool.

'No,' she says, grabbing my arm. 'Say one word and I'll tell them all you were down here perving on me last night. Yeah,' she adds with a nasty grin. 'I saw you.'

I reach for her fingers and remove them from my arm. 'Go on then,' I say, calling her bluff. 'You tell them that. Then I can tell them what you were doing down here. I'm sure your mum would love to know more about those photos you were taking.'

She holds my stare, defiant, yet her eyes give away too much. She is unsettled. She won't do it.

'What's the pill, Georgia?'

'It's mine,' she says, her voice thin, less self-assured now. She falls silent, as though that alone will be enough to persuade me that her intentions moments ago were innocent. 'It's just a headache tablet, that's all.'

Her eyes plead with me not to say anything. I glance behind me. Toni is at the far end of the pool, engrossed in conversation with Martha. Claire is swimming lengths. Holly and Zoe are at the near side, Holly's attention caught by Georgia and me as Zoe chatters away to her, oblivious.

'Swallow it then.'

'What?'

'You said it's yours. So take it.'

She narrows her eyes at me. 'I'll take it later.' When she tries to pass me, I sidestep her, blocking her way. 'Take it. Or I'll go and tell everyone you were about to spike Holly's drink. I'll tell them about the photos too.'

'Fuck off,' she whispers through gritted teeth, but her eyes fill with tears and she knows she is trapped.

'Okay. Your choice.' I turn to the pool.

'No, don't.' She grabs my arm. Holly is watching us. 'It's nothing, okay? Just a headache tablet, that's all.'

I wait and say nothing; she knows what I want her to do. If it is nothing, she will swallow it. It won't harm her, will it? She turns and takes a glass at random, pausing for a moment before raising it to her lips. Then she puts the tablet on her tongue before swallowing it. She allows herself to meet my eye, and in hers I see the panic that has risen in her pupils.

'I hope it helps your head.'

She sets the glass back down and leaves without a word. She is probably going to the toilet to make herself sick. I've seen enough painkillers in my time to know that whatever Georgia was about to put in that drink, it wasn't a remedy for a headache.

I pick up my own champagne glass and empty it.

'Is everything okay?' Holly stands beside me, dripping water onto the tiles at our feet. She is shivering.

'Fine. Georgia said she's got a bit of a headache. Are you cold? It's chilly, isn't it? I think I'll go and get my robe. Do you need anything from the bedroom?'

She shakes her head, her eyes still resting on me as though she doesn't trust me. And why would she? She has every reason not to. She doesn't realise it yet, but I doubt there is a single person among us Holly should trust.

THIRTEEN

Claire

After everyone has finished at the pool, we go upstairs to get showered and dressed. I splash my face with cold water in the en suite. In the bottom of my washbag is the box of Xanax I double-checked I had packed before leaving the house yesterday. I study it for a moment, deliberating over the combination of drug and alcohol, knowing that I won't be able to dodge the latter now that cocktail-making is about to begin downstairs. It will just take the edge off, I tell myself. It'll be fine.

Knowing it probably isn't the best of ideas, I put a tablet on my tongue and wash it down with tap water. I need something to take me from this place while I'm still stuck here; something that will ease the thought of what I'll be going home to. I have to escape myself somehow, if only for the rest of today. I wish it was so easy to escape everyone else here too.

I hear Zoe come into the bedroom, and when I go to get changed, I'm forced to make small talk, as though everything is normal. I can't bring myself to look at her. I know it was Aaron's car I saw her getting out of in the lane; I think her staged sickness this morning was a deliberate ploy to stay back at the house alone. But why was Aaron here? My heart wants to believe that he has organised a surprise for Holly, with Zoe's help, but I know this is a ridiculous hope. If he had wanted to arrange anything, to contribute to the weekend in some way, he would have consulted Martha first, or even me. And what husband-to-be does that anyway, involving himself with his partner's hen weekend?

He didn't come here, did he? Surely Zoe wouldn't have let him, knowing that Georgia was still in the house?

When I think of last night, of when we all sat together in the living room and watched the video recording Aaron made for Holly, Zoe's reactions replay on a loop. Something changed in her as soon as she saw him. Why did she get up and leave the room in the way she did? And she'd done the same thing earlier in the day, when we were all in the steam room together, claiming to be too hot as soon as Holly started discussing Aaron's stag weekend. I don't want to have to share a room with her again tonight, not now I know what she's been up to.

I think of Holly chatting with her in the pool, blissfully unaware of what's going on behind her back. Why would Aaron do this to her? They're not even married yet, and if he wanted to be with someone else, why not just call off the wedding? I suppose that's not what affairs are all about, though; the adulterer doesn't usually want to be with the person they're being unfaithful with, not in the way they are already with their spouse. The other person is a distraction from real life, a source of excitement; a catalyst of the kind of danger that seems provocative until it implodes.

How can Zoe behave like this, be in the same room as Holly, join her for her hen weekend, knowing what she has been doing? What she is apparently still doing.

And yet I know I am a hypocrite for even having this thought. Aren't I sitting among people too – my friends – silent with my own secrets?

Downstairs, everyone has dressed to impress, as instructed on Martha's itinerary. The dress code is 'glam' and Toni has certainly taken it literally, glittering like a disco ball in a tiny sequinned minidress that looks as though it might have been borrowed from Georgia's wardrobe. Holly is classy and under-stated as always in a black tea dress accessorised with beautiful silver jewellery, while Martha wears a floor-length strapless gold gown, looking like she's about to present an award at a music ceremony. Yet again I find myself feeling frumpy and old next to everyone else, self-conscious in the berry-red skater dress I pulled from the back of the wardrobe, unworn in years. It is a little too tight for me, the baby weight still clinging in all the wrong places, and I regret now not buying myself something new for the occasion. I couldn't justify the expense.

On the island at the centre of the kitchen is a collection of spirits, fruit juices and soft drinks, all of us having brought something different to contribute to the cocktail-making. I feel a headache coming on already, the champagne and the Xanax creating their own toxic cocktail in my gut. Outside, snow is still falling. We might all get stuck here. No chance of heading home early tomorrow, and if that's to be the case anyway, oblivion seems an appealing option. When do I ever allow myself to let go?

'Right,' Martha says, holding up a bottle of gin as though it's an Olympic torch. 'Everyone mix themselves a drink. We're playing Never Have I Ever.'

There are groans from a couple of us, although Holly and Suzanne seem strangely enthusiastic about the idea. Perhaps they are the only people in the room who feel confident they have nothing to hide, or at the very least nothing that might cause them embarrassment were it to be exposed.

'We're not thirteen,' I say, common sense replacing the uncharacteristic thoughts that have just danced through my brain. 'Is that a good idea?'

'Why not?' Martha challenges. 'What have you done?' She laughs before eyeing me mockingly. 'Never have I ever gone to bed without having a mug of Bovril first. Oops... shot for Claire.'

'Stop it,' Holly says playfully. 'The problem is, Claire, Martha knows she's going to be having a drink after every question.'

Martha opens her mouth in mock horror before casting Holly a sickly-sweet smile.

We take our drinks and go into the living room, where Toni lights a fire in the beautiful open fireplace. It feels cosy and comforting, but I know this setting is a smokescreen for everything that lies beneath the surface of what is visible.

'Who wants to start us off then? Zoe?'

It couldn't have been a worse choice of person, I think. I sip my drink, a cosmopolitan, and watch Zoe, wondering what she might come up with.

'God,' she says. 'I haven't played this in years. Okay... never have I ever... been skinny-dipping.'

Martha groans. 'Playing it safe, I see.' She takes a drink. 'Who hasn't ever done that?'

'I haven't,' Suzanne says.

'Really?' Martha smiles. 'What a wasted youth. There's a swimming pool here, remember... first time for everything. Your question next then.'

Suzanne's mouth curls at the corner as she considers a question. 'Never have I ever...' There is a long pause, made uncomfortable by the way her eyes dart between each of us, assessing the possible revelations that might be exposed by whatever she is contemplating. 'Lied about my age.'

Despite the game setting my nerves on edge – or perhaps it's just the onset of the Xanax and the cocktail – I find myself oddly disappointed by the tameness of the question. The mood feels almost dangerous, the threat that someone may reveal too much of themselves lingering in the air like an unspoken promise. With an enthusiasm I know isn't gracious, I find myself thinking that I don't mind who it happens to, as long as it's not me.

Everyone takes a drink, and the shared response momentarily lightens the mood. There are a couple more questions before the focus falls on me, by which time, I have mine ready.

'Never have I ever been unfaithful.'

Martha pulls a pained expression, her lips pursing into a tight circle. 'Awkward.'

I wait to see who will be honest, but not a single woman raises a glass to her lips. Zoe's attention has turned to Holly, and I notice something flicker between the two of them, some silent communication that seems to go unnoticed by everyone else. Surely Holly doesn't know? It's impossible; if she did, she would never have brought Zoe here this weekend.

'Everyone's so well behaved,' I say, feeling my lip curl with sarcasm that is intended to be noticed.

Holly changes the subject quickly, asking a safer-than-safe question about travelling alone. As the game goes on, each person continues in the same vein, carefully editing the subjects their questions cover, assessing the mood before voicing their turn. Martha appears increasingly on edge, twitchy and impatient. She keeps checking her phone, though few of us have managed to get a signal for longer than a few minutes since arriving yesterday. She makes frequent visits to the hallway while the rest of us chat in the living room, trying to pace ourselves between questions and going to the kitchen for top-ups of cocktails. At this rate, I'll be ready for bed by 7.30.

The game has been abandoned and Georgia has come downstairs to join us when Martha reappears in the living room doorway.

'Seems a shame, doesn't it?' she says, leaning dramatically against the door frame, her head tilted so that her hair falls in a curtain at her side. 'All these drinks and no one to serve them.'

She gives Holly a smile before stepping to one side. Behind her, a man appears.

'God, Martha,' I say quietly, though loud enough for him to hear. 'You're joking me.'

He's wearing nothing, the man in the doorway – well, nothing other than a black apron, a pair of sliders and a stupid smile.

'Anyone in need of a waiter, ladies?' His accent is thick West Country and doesn't seem to fit with the rest of him somehow.

In the corner, from behind the screen of her iPhone, Georgia sniggers. 'Cringefest,' she mutters.

I am seething. Holly is all smiles, but of course she would be; she has always put everyone else's feelings above her own, and she wouldn't want to upset Martha by doing anything to suggest that this was a stupid idea. This is not for Holly, I think; this is for Martha, another ridiculous gimmick she can photograph and filter before posting on Instagram. Look what an amazing friend I am. Look how much fun we're having.

'Let's all go through to the kitchen,' she suggests, ignoring the look I give her.

I stand and step into the hallway, grabbing her by the arm as she turns to follow the man into the other room. 'This is one surprise too many, don't you think?'

'Chill out, Claire,' she says, shaking her arm from my grip. 'What are you afraid of, that you might actually start enjoying yourself?'

Our exchange is cut short when the others emerge from the living room. Whatever animosity exists between Martha and me, it must wait to be aired beyond the walls of this building, somewhere without an audience.

Martha tosses her hair over her shoulder and ushers everyone into the kitchen, ever the attentive hostess. On so many occasions I've wondered whether she hates me. Now I realise that isn't the case at all. It is me who despises her; I've just never wanted to admit it.

FOURTEEN

Suzanne

Martha ushers us all into the kitchen, where the butler-in-the-buff introduces himself as Sean before launching into a full-blown Tom Cruise-esque performance of bottle flipping and spirit mixing. It is meant as just a bit of fun, I'm sure, but it is obvious from Claire's reaction that she doesn't see it as such. She waits a moment in the hallway before joining the rest of us, her expression soured by whatever words have just been exchanged between her and Martha. Outside, the snow is falling thicker and faster, though no one seems to pay it much attention. As the afternoon creeps into evening and the skies darken further, the scene that lies outside the doors is eerily beautiful.

It is beautiful, but it will keep us trapped here.

The others are laughing about something now; when I look over, I see a packet of flesh-coloured penis-shaped plastic straws being passed around by Toni, who puts one in her mouth and poses provocatively before passing it to a horrified-looking Claire, who drops it on the floor. Of course, no one else here seems to realise just how natural this type of pose is for Toni; or if they are aware, no one makes any mention of it, protecting her from possible embarrassment or shame. I wonder why she does it, why she sells those photographs of herself to strangers online, so revealing and so degrading. By all accounts her business is doing well, so I can't imagine it's for the money.

No one could find the account easily, not unless they were specifically searching Toni out online. She doesn't use her real name on the profile, adopting a pseudonym that would keep her hidden from any online search. But there was a link on her bakery's Instagram account that inadvertently led me to her OnlyFans page – a comment left by another woman who also has an account on the site. I didn't believe it when I saw it at first. I had to return to her social media profiles to look at other photographs, double-checking that this really was her, but I'd made no mistake. Georgia cannot possibly know about it. How humiliating it would be for a teenager to find out that her mother sells semi-nude photographs of herself – and perhaps more – to strangers on the internet.

'Suzanne. You're lagging behind.' Martha grabs my hand, her fingers cold against mine. She reaches to the island, where Sean is mixing drinks and chatting with Holly, Claire and Toni, passing me a glass filled with a lurid blue concoction. 'I promise you,' she says, 'it'll be the best thing you've ever tasted.'

I take a drink; she is right, it really is delicious, though I've no idea what the cocktail is made up of. I trust Martha, though whether or not that is wise is yet to be seen. She has a quality about her that invites solidarity, despite her apparently hard edges.

Behind us, Claire is talking erratically, her speech slurring and her words muddled. It started in the living room earlier, but is becoming more pronounced now, her behaviour increasingly manic.

'Is she okay?' I ask quietly.

Martha rolls her eyes and waves a hand dismissively. 'Can't handle her drink.'

Sean keeps glancing through the patio doors. The snow is falling faster now, the lawn a sheet of ghostly white beneath the glow of the outdoor lights. I see him look at the oversized clock on the far wall, presumably wondering whether he'll be able to make it home by the time his booking finishes. I've no idea how long Martha has paid to have him here; the very thought that she has purchased a person to serve us drinks while wearing next to nothing seems increasingly seedy and tacky the more I think about it. It is something I could never imagine Holly wanting for her hen weekend, though she's playing along politely, smiling and laughing in all the right places.

'I don't think I can stay until seven,' I hear Sean say to Martha. 'Look at it.' He gestures to the window. In the half-light, evening seems to have crept up on us even earlier than it did last night, the snow coming down thick and fast.

'We'll all be stuck here at this rate,' I say.

'We've got the place booked until Monday anyway,' Martha says with a shrug. 'Worst-case scenario we have to stay another night.'

'Says the self-employed one,' Claire slurs. 'It's not that straightforward for the rest of us.' She gets up from her bar stool but misses her footing and falls forward. Holly grabs her before she can hit her head against the island.

'Are you okay?' Sean asks, as Holly redirects a drunken Claire to the stool.

'Fine. I'm fine. You're very good. Isn't he kind?' she says, turning to Holly.

Holly casts Martha a look that appeals for help. Claire's drunken state has taken a quick turn; despite her generally erratic behaviour, she didn't seem nearly so bad just half an hour ago. Now she's struggling to stay upright, swaying as though the gentlest of nudges would knock her over.

'Are you married?' she asks Sean. 'I mean, I am, but I may as well not be, do you know what I mean? He's a useless prick. *She's* getting married.' She puts a hand on Holly's arm, leaning against her to keep herself from falling for a second time. 'Aaron. He's nice, isn't he? He's a keeper. Like you said last night, Suzanne, too good to be true. What do you think, Zoe?'

'About what?'

'About Aaron,' Claire says, managing to drag his name across four syllables. 'He can't be as perfect as he seems, can he?'

'I—'

'Come on, Zoe,' Claire urges, not giving her a chance to respond. 'There must be something he's keeping hidden, mustn't there? No one's that perfect.'

'For God's sake, Claire,' Martha says. 'What's got into you?' She turns and reaches for an empty glass, holding it up to illustrate her point. 'Other than twenty cosmopolitans,' she mutters. She goes to the sink and fills the glass with water before handing it to Claire. 'Drink that.'

'I'm not drunk.' Claire takes the glass and puts it down, too hard, on the marble worktop in front of her. It shatters as it leaves her hand, tiny shards spraying everywhere like macabre confetti.

'Claire!' Holly rushes to her aid; Claire's hand is bleeding. Holly takes it in hers, searching around for something to staunch the flow.

'It's fine,' Claire objects, pulling away. 'It's just a scratch.'

I pass Holly the first thing that comes to hand, a tea towel that's been left on the back of one of the stools. She reaches for Claire again and closes it around her bleeding palm, resisting her attempts to wrangle her arm free. Claire eventually wins, though, and when she yanks away from Holly, she turns sharply, almost losing her balance.

'I'm fine,' she says again. 'I'm fine.'

Then she staggers from the room, leaving the rest of us in an awkward silence that is finally broken when Sean declares that it is time for him to leave.

FIFTEEN

Holly

After Claire disappears upstairs, Sean departs. The evening outside is chillingly perfect: dense snow, untouched by human or animal, lies unbroken in a thick rug that stretches to the darkened reaches of the garden, and the air has a cleanliness about it, pure and unpolluted, tricking me into thinking that I could be somewhere in a remote corner of the earth. I am beginning to wish I was. The weekend has taken some unprecedented turns, and with Suzanne's lie and Claire's erratic behaviour having dominated the day, I'm beginning to wish that the weekend could somehow be cut short.

I miss Aaron. Though I saw him only a little over twenty-four hours ago, it feels that I've been away from home for much longer, and I miss the comforts of the life we've built around one another. Perhaps I've taken it for granted, failing to realise just how precious an existence it is. I am lucky. Luckier than perhaps I deserve.

We're clearing up the mess in the kitchen, returning caps to spirit bottles and wiping up spills; sweeping up the broken glass that's all over the floor. Claire's erratic behaviour is easily explained, though I'm the only one who knows this. I'm not sure how many cocktails she had, but I don't think it's enough to have caused her slurred speech and disorientation. My guess is that at some point today – probably when we got back from the pub – she took some Xanax. Combined with the alcohol in her system, it's clearly having a dangerous effect. I should go upstairs and check she hasn't taken any more since she left the kitchen. If she's using it in the hope that it will makes things better for her, it's already obvious it won't.

As the others head for the living room, I go to the downstairs bathroom. When I come back out, Martha is in the hallway waiting for me.

'What the fuck is up with Claire?' she asks, her voice lowered to a whisper. 'If she wasn't such a square, I'd think she'd taken something.'

It's not my business to discuss Claire's personal life with Martha, or with anyone, so I say nothing. When she's ready to confide in us she will. I usher Martha into the bathroom and close the door to keep out any prying ears that might be lurking.

'Go easy on her,' I say. 'There are things she's struggling with at the moment.'

'What things?'

I raise an eyebrow, a signal for her to not ask me anything more. The hurt on her face is apparent in an instant; she sees Claire and me as united somehow, separating ourselves with our secrets, and I know this is a continuation of the resentment she feels at me having chosen Claire as maid of honour over her. I didn't expect her to be so sensitive. It makes me wonder whether I know her as well as I've always thought I do.

'It's a shame not everyone has gone easy on her then,' she says, looking down at her phone.

'What do you mean?'

She taps and scrolls before finding what she's looking for and passing me the phone.

'They say a photograph never lies, don't they?' she says. 'But this one certainly does.'

My heart sinks as I look at the image on the screen. It is a cruel example of just how manipulative the camera can be. The person responsible for tapping a finger to freeze the moment doesn't need to be involved in the deceit; sometimes a bad angle and an ill-timed movement from the subject in focus can tell their own lie, completely unaided. But I know whose finger snapped this shot, and I know that Georgia intended for it to be as damning as it appears.

'She's posted this on Instagram?'

Martha nods. 'Sean asked me to leave him a review on social media. Georgia's used the hashtag "hen party". I'm not sure this is the kind of endorsement he was after.'

In the image, Sean is standing with his back to the camera, mixing drinks at the island in the centre of the kitchen. With only a short black apron to cover his modesty, his backside is completely on show. I feel uncomfortable looking at the photograph; he had no idea it was being taken. It feels intrusive and disrespectful, a breach of trust. An image for which he offered no permission is now floating online, available for viewing by anyone who might happen to see it.

But it is Claire I feel most sorry for. She appears in the foreground, little more than a few inches behind Sean if the photograph is to be taken at face value. In truth, I know this wasn't the case, and what is seen in this image is a falsehood: it never happened. But no one looking at it who wasn't here at this house today would ever believe this to be the case. If Gareth was to see it, he would never believe any story other than the one the photograph tells.

Claire is leaning down. She might have been picking something up off the floor, and when I cast my mind back to the last couple of hours, I realise that's exactly what she was doing. The straw she dropped when Toni passed it to her. She was bending to pick it up. But the photograph doesn't show that. The straw is barely visible, only noticeable to someone who knew it was there. What the photograph shows is Claire leaning forward with her face turned directly to Sean's naked arse. The positioning of them both, along with the unfortunate perspective, makes it look as though her nose is just inches from his flesh. It might be funny in some other context, if both subjects were in on the joke and the image had not been posted on the internet, the action intentionally damaging.

'What a little bitch, right?' Martha raises an eyebrow. 'I'm sorry, Holly, I know you don't want me to say it, but that girl is trouble. She should never have come here this weekend. I'm starting to think she has some kind of hidden agenda.'

'Like what?' I challenge her. 'Honestly, Martha, I know Georgia is hard work, but she's a teenager – they're all the same. Caleb's no different.' I give the phone back to her. 'We need to get her to take it down.'

Martha blows air through her teeth. 'That'll be Toni's job.'

'Fine. We'd better let her know then.'

Martha locks her phone and puts it on the windowsill. 'For fuck's sake,' she mutters.

'What?'

'This is a total fuck-up. This weekend was supposed to be about you.'

I am almost grateful for the interruption when the bathroom door bursts open, though my first thought is that I should have locked it when I closed it. It's Claire, and the way she bumps against the frame on her way in only confirms that my suspicions are correct. The combination of medication, which she is usually so opposed to, and alcohol, when she rarely drinks, has been too much for her.

'Why didn't you tell me about Sean?' she asks Martha, who rolls her eyes at Claire's challenging tone.

'Here we go again. Not everything's about you, Claire. It was meant to be a surprise.'

'It was certainly that.' Claire turns to me. 'Did you enjoy it?'

I don't know what the right answer is to that, and a mere moment of hesitation is enough to fuel her apparent search for an argument. 'No. There we are, Martha. No one wanted it. Only you, apparently.'

'You've had too much to drink.'

Claire's eyes widen. 'What are you now, my mother?'

It is a poor choice of phrase, one that triggers a reaction in Martha. Tension pulls at her features, though she manages to swallow whatever words might be on the tip of her tongue.

'Why did you bring Zoe this weekend?' Claire asks me, her eyes narrowed.

The question is sudden and random. I look to Martha for help, but she seems as confused by Claire's behaviour as I am.

'She's a friend.'

Claire blows air through her teeth, making a sound that mocks my declaration. 'Zoe is no friend of yours, Holly,' she slurs. 'Just know that, okay? Please know that.'

'Come on,' I say, putting an arm around her shoulders. 'You need to sit down.'

'Don't do that!' She swipes my arm away, and for a moment I don't know which one of us is more surprised by her violent reaction. 'I'm not drunk,' she objects, her words blurring into one another again. And I believe her. This is the Xanax. The slurred speech, the confusion, the paranoia – they are all side effects of the medication.

'She's lying to you,' she says, tapping a finger on my chest. 'Ask her about Aaron.'

NOW

SUNDAY

In films, drowning is often depicted as a peaceful death, endowing the victim with a macabre and eerie beauty that suggests they found some calm in the act. A woman's hair strewn like seaweed just below the surface of the water, framing her face before she's pulled into the depths. Wide eyes stare out, silently accepting.

In truth, it is far from peaceful. The reality is violent and terrifying, the process painful and drawn out, she knows that. The fear, she thinks. How excruciating, that panic as the lungs fill and the timer set within the brain counts down as time quickly fades to nothing.

Is this how she died? She was here, and yet she wasn't. She can't remember. She isn't sure of anything any more. Nothing looks the way it should.

Behind her, someone's speaking on the phone. The words are muted and muffled as though she's the one who is underwater, each word blurred into the next as they empty a tirade of panic onto the listener at the other end of the line. The room seems to move around her, the others passing in a frenzy that has been somehow slowed, time stalling, torturing her by making her watch every unfolding moment in slow motion.

'What did you do to her?'

She looks up; she has no choice. But the words aren't directed at her, and she feels a relief swell in her chest that she knows is ill-timed and inappropriate.

'I didn't do anything. I haven't seen her since we were all together earlier.'

'Everyone saw what happened between you. Did you do this to her?'

God, the cry of pain that escapes her. It is the worst sound she has ever heard, primeval and raw.

'Stop it, please.'

'No one knows what happened.'

'Let's just wait until someone gets here.'

'Stop telling me what to fucking do!'

Their words crash over one another, their voices rising to a crescendo until they break into oblivion, her brain silencing them with a switch flicked for self-preservation.

She was in the water.

She was in the water.

She drowned.

But this can't be how any of it happened, can it? She knows this for a fact, because when she left her, when she last saw her lying here on these tiles, she was already dead. Wasn't she?

SIX HOURS EARLIER

SIXTEEN

Claire

This is ruined, we are ruined, everything's over now. My head hurts. The Xanax. The cocktails. The lights hurt my eyes. And what I said... I wish I'd never said it. What did I say?

Zoe. I said something about Zoe. No friend... that was it. Oh God, I told her to ask Zoe about Aaron. As soon as I'd said it, I wished I hadn't. Whatever's happened, whatever is going on, this is supposed to be Holly's weekend. Between us, we are ruining it. But what sort of hen weekend is this if one of the so-called friends is having some sort of affair with the husband-to-be? The whole thing is a farce. The liars. The lied-to. The keepers of secrets.

I'm beginning to wonder whether there's a single person here Holly can trust.

I'll tell her what I have done when we get home, but not here. I will tell her everything. It will be cathartic, a detox; I will feel better for the truth finally being out in the open, no longer the sole carrier of the burden that's weighed upon me. I will tell Zoe that I know what she's been up to, and that she needs to be the one to tell Holly the truth.

I should have gone up to bed, but instead I've come to the pool room, the only place where I can escape everyone else and be by myself. The room is dark, the water still and shimmering. I take off my socks and roll up my pyjamas, sitting at the pool edge to dip my legs into the water. I wonder what Holly and Martha are doing now. I imagine that if Holly hasn't already gone to question Zoe about what I said, Martha will be doing it for her.

I lean forward towards the pool, my reflection a darkened blob on the surface of the water. Just a blur. Perhaps this is me; this is what I have become.

When I was younger, I thought about killing myself. It was an invasive thought that broke through my consciousness, an unexpected arrival at a party it hadn't been invited to, and though I knew that it was a dangerous distraction from all the things I needed to remind myself of and keep my focus on, I allowed the visitor to stay in my brain, meeting with it occasionally to discuss the possibility. It felt inappropriately comforting somehow, like knowing where the exit points were should there happen to be a fire.

Then I had the boys, and everything changed. In those first seconds of holding my oldest son against my chest, my life was no longer about me. I was the sole provider, the depended-upon. Everything I would go on to do would be for them, and it is. It always will be. I can forgive myself with that thought, and I need to, often. Every decision I make, I do with my children's best interests at heart. Even the ones that mean someone else may inevitably have to suffer.

A thought flashes into my brain, intrusive and alarming. Myself, face down in the pool, my body weighty and bloated, floating just beneath the surface of the water. The image makes me giddy and I have to stop myself from falling forwards, my body pulling itself towards the imagining as though wanting to make it a reality.

When Toni comes into the room, I am still fighting to catch my breath. She must wonder why I am gasping, and when she sits down next to me I am ashamed of myself beside her. I'm frumpy and unfit; I've let myself go. I'm going to look ridiculous in my bridesmaid dress standing alongside the others.

I have wondered in recent months whether I would have been less angry with Gareth if he'd had an affair, and when I allow myself an honest response, the truth is that yes, it would have hurt me less. I have let myself go, and sex would have been something I could have understood, if not overlooked; I might have blamed myself as much as I blamed him. But the gambling has felt like the worst of betrayals, something I had no control over and couldn't have prevented from happening. He has cheated all of us, the boys and me.

Beside me, Toni leans back and looks up at the stars embedded in the ceiling. The ring in her nose glints in the darkness, and when she catches me looking, she gives me a smile. 'You okay?'

'Yeah, I'm okay. You?'

She shrugs. Of course she's not okay. None of us is okay, and those who say we are are just lying to ourselves.

Her entire weekend must have been consumed with thoughts of Georgia. Georgia can't have told her who the baby's father is; if she had, I imagine that would surely have come out by now. History is repeating itself, and Toni must feel powerless to prevent it. Despite all her flaws and her angst, despite her anger and her violence, Georgia is still, in so many ways, just a child.

'I feel like we've made up for lost time this weekend,' Toni says, putting a hand on my arm. 'It's been nice.'

Panic rises in my chest. As it gathers in my throat, I feel as though I might suffocate. The surface of the pool seems to move somehow, as though a shiver has passed through it. It's reminding me that it is still there, that it is still a possibility.

'Toni.'

'Yeah?'

But I can't say it. I will never be able to say it. I wonder how relationships manage to exist when they are embroiled in secrets, because they do – there is evidence of them everywhere. Affairs that are never admitted to, paternity that's concealed, lies that are repeated over and over until the person who has uttered them either grows comfortable with their own dishonesty or starts to believe that the falsehood has at least some grounding in fact.

'What's the matter?'

'Nothing,' I say.

Toni takes a deep breath before exhaling long and loud, tilting her head back as though meditating. 'I wonder how much Martha paid for that butler-in-the-buff.'

'No wonder she didn't ask us first. She must have known we would never have agreed to it.'

She lifts an arm to gesture to the room. 'Look at this place. As if it only cost two hundred quid each.'

'Martha's already said she doesn't want anything extra.'

'That's not the point, though, is it? I don't want to be in her debt. I don't want to be in anyone's debt.'

A line of sweat has gathered at the back of my neck. I put a hand to it and wipe it away, hating its uncomfortable warmth on my fingertips. 'I thought everything was going well with the business?'

'It is. I mean, as well as it can, you know, all things considered. It's not the business.' She exhales loudly. 'There's something else.'

And before I can say anything – before I am able to think of a way to distract her somehow, or find an excuse that will mean we both have to get up and leave – she begins to cry. I've never seen her cry before. Toni's not a crier. She's a swearer, the giver of a cold shoulder; a time-to-herself lover of the silent treatment. I have known her to mutter profanities beneath her breath, and to speak them aloud when the mood has taken her; I have seen her slam doors on the exit of an argument. But I have never seen her break down. I have never had to look at her tears, and I cannot bring myself to look at them now.

'Fuck,' she says suddenly, slapping a hand to her head as though batting away an errant wasp, or trying to beat out an unwanted thought. 'Fuck, fuck, fuck.'

'Stop it,' I say, because I can think of nothing else; she is unsettling me a bit, her anger misplaced and random; my own brain too addled by the Xanax and the cocktails to make any sense of her outburst. 'Is this about what you told me?'

'I need your help, Claire.'

Of all the things she might have said to me, this somehow seems the worst. I cannot help her. I don't want to help her. I should want to, I should be better than I am, but I am in no position to help anyone, not when my own life is such a chaotic shambles.

'Toni—'

'I've done something terrible,' she sobs, looking at me through her thick fringe, her eyes red-rimmed; her face pale and ghost-like.

Don't tell me. Don't tell me.

'I don't think—'

'Please,' she says, holding my arm too tightly, cutting my words short for a second time. 'I just need to tell someone and I don't know who else to turn to. I know I shouldn't be doing this now, not this weekend, but I've let things go too far and now they're out of control. Have you ever felt like everything has just slipped from your grip?' And then she laughs, the sound bordering on manic even to my drug-addled brain. 'Of course you haven't. Reliable, organised, hard-working Claire... you've always got everything under control. How do you do it? How do you juggle everything in the way you do, keeping everyone and everything afloat? Without you, the whole ship and everyone on it goes under, that's how it works, isn't it? At home, with us four, probably at work too, am I right? Everything falls apart without you. You're the anchor. You the thing that's keeping us steady. Without you, the rest of us would drown.'

She is still clutching my arm, her fingertips digging into my flesh and her knuckles whitened with the effort. She's charged and manic in a way I have never seen her. She has had more to drink than I realised, although I've not been focusing on anyone else's consumption – not even on my own.

Noticing my focus upon her fingers, on the flesh that has paled to white beneath their force, she releases her grip.

'I'm not as in control as you think I am, Toni. No one's lives are what other people think they are, not really.' If only you knew, I think.

'I'm sorry. I'm just desperate, Claire. I don't know where else to turn.'

Don't tell me. Don't tell me. The words repeat in a cycle, increasing in intensity and speed and volume with each rotation of my brain until I can almost believe that I am screaming them aloud. *Don't tell me.*

'I did something, Claire. Something fucking terrible that I've never been able to tell anyone.'

Someone bursts through the door, bringing the conversation to an abrupt stop. I have never been more grateful for an interruption. I have never been more grateful to see Georgia.

'What are you talking about?'

Toni laughs awkwardly. 'Hello to you too, dear daughter. Why? Did you want to join us?'

Georgia pulls a face and glances at me with contempt. 'No thanks.' Her head jerks to one side; I can't tell whether it's intentional or some kind of nervous tic. Her eyes seem to be dancing, unable to rest their focus upon any single point. 'Can I speak to you?' she says to her mother. 'Alone.'

Toni sighs and stands. She follows Georgia to the door before turning back to me. 'Don't stay in here on your own,' she tells me. 'It's getting cold.'

I watch them leave, then exhale noisily, relief pouring from me in a wave of warm breath. Toni wanted to confess something to me, and I am not so good an actress that I could have faked ignorance – not this time. The thing is, I already know her secret. She is ready to crack – doesn't everyone have their breaking point? And when she finds out what I'm responsible for, I will be the last person she ever wants to confide in.

SEVENTEEN

Holly

In the bedroom, Claire's words circle on an endless loop inside my brain. She's drunk, I tell myself. Her judgement has been affected by the medication. She has no idea what she's saying. And yet the more I consider the possibility of her insinuation, the more I recall the details of Zoe's behaviour yesterday: leaving the steam room after talk of Aaron's stag do; leaving the living room after watching the video he made for me. Could I believe it of her? Perhaps. I don't know. We haven't known each other for very long, not in the way I know the others. Maybe she isn't who I think she is.

But Aaron? No, I can't believe it of him.

When Suzanne comes into the bedroom, I leave to get a glass of water, barely acknowledging her as we pass. She's been speaking to me normally all evening, behaving as though she's a friend like any other, but try as I might, I cannot shake the knowledge that she isn't. In truth, I'm not sure that I know who she is at all. I have tried in as many ways as possible to explain the woman at the other end of the phone this morning – the woman who responded to the word 'Mum' – as someone whose existence doesn't sever my friendship with Suzanne in half, but I am always brought back to the same thought. She has lied. She is a liar.

Her mother isn't dead.

I must confront what I know, but I don't want to do it here, not in front of the others, and not where we are so isolated. I want to be on home ground, the conversation had on my own terms. I want to be certain that I haven't made a mistake, yet I already know in my heart and my head that there is no other reasoning for what has happened. But what I can't explain to myself is why she would do it, why she would lie to me about something so huge for all these years.

On the landing, I see Toni; she has been crying, her dark make-up smudged beneath her eyes. 'What's happened?' I ask.

'I'm fine,' she lies. 'Honestly. Too much alcohol. Nothing a good sleep won't fix.' She moves towards me, holds me in a sudden and unexpected embrace, and it is so unlike her that I don't know how to respond. 'I love you, Holly.'

I laugh awkwardly. 'You're right,' I tell her, easing her from me. 'You've definitely had too much alcohol. What's the matter? Is it Georgia? Look, if you want to talk about why she had to come here this weekend, I—'

She shakes her head. 'Everything's fine. I'll see you in the morning, okay?'

She goes into her bedroom and I head downstairs, my throat dry with thirst. It is dark, but not so dark that I fail to notice that there's a stranger in the house. A man.

I see him when I go into the kitchen, a thick bulk that disappears into the corridor leading from the house to the pool room. My fingers tighten around the stem of my glass, preparing it as a weapon. The beating of my heart is suddenly so loud that I fear it will draw attention to me. Where is everyone? It was definitely a man: tall, wearing dark clothing and a beanie hat.

I don't turn on the light, fearful that he might notice it and come back. My heart races as I panic over what I should do next, knowing there's no time for deliberation. I should go and find one of the others, but other than Toni, I don't know where anyone is. One of them might be in the spa, unaware that there's a man in there. By the time I get back here with someone else, anything might have happened. I'd be guilty of doing nothing.

I go to the drawers at the far side of the kitchen and pull out the biggest knife I can find, my hand shaking with the possibility of what it might be used for. Whether I am capable.

The corridor is steeped in darkness. There is a light switch somewhere, but I dare not grope about for it, not wanting to be seen. Not wanting to see. I know that beyond these walls there's over a foot of snow, possibly more by now. It would be impossible for someone to have arrived here now, by car or on foot. My thoughts revert to the butler-in-the-buff, Sean. What if he didn't leave? What if he has been here for these past few hours, watching us, waiting?

I stand with my back to the wall and take a deep breath. I am being ridiculous, allowing my mind to race to the craziest of conclusions. Sean left; Martha went to the door with him. She would have seen him go. Besides, I'm sure he wasn't as tall as the man I've just spotted, his figure shorter and stockier.

But if it isn't him, then who have I just seen? How long has he been here?

The door to the pool room has been left open; there's a light on in there. It's cold in the corridor, a draught cutting through the space as I stalk to the spa like a thief. The spotlights are turned on. At the pool, tiny stars are reflected on the dark surface of the water. The knife's handle feels cold against my palm, and a shiver races through me. It is useless, I know. I don't think I could ever use it. I don't think I am capable of hurting another person, even in the most extreme of circumstances.

I push the door wider. The room is silent – unsettlingly so. My feet feel leaden, weighted to the floor, and as I wait for something – anything – to happen, I hear the rhythmic drip of a shower that hasn't been turned off fully. And then I hear something else. A low groan. A moan. A woman's voice.

I don't have time to consider the danger. I cross the pool room and follow the sound, my palm, hot and sweaty despite the cold, gripped around the knife handle. The steam room is on. The glass door is frosted and opaque, but I can see movement within, more than one person inside.

I stand at the door, my heart pounding. 'I know you're in there,' I say, frustrated by the ridiculousness of my voice, the stupidity of my words. I hear a woman's voice, muffled, and then there is silence. A scene from a horror film plays out in my mind – a pale throat, white knuckles, pink water trailing down a plughole. With a shove that sends the door crashing into whoever is behind it, I burst into the damp, hot air of the steam room, grabbing the man by the arm, the knife in my free hand flailing blindly.

'What are you doing? Stop it!'

Not my words, but his. An arm is raised, the knife is knocked from my hand; it is too late. I look down, see the blood in the water at my feet.

'Jesus, Mum! What have you done?'

EIGHTEEN

Suzanne

I find Martha in her room, getting changed. She's left the door ajar, and through the gap I watch her remove her dress, her shoulder blades flexing as she works her slender arms through the straps. She is ageless somehow – unchanged – time removing nothing from her, only seeming to have added good things, gifting her special extras with every passing year.

She slips on the nightdress she wore yesterday, assessing herself in the mirror as I did last night, turning from one side to the other, scanning every angle. To everyone else, she appears the picture of confidence and success. Zoe is in awe of her wealth and her possessions, while Claire is jealous of everything Martha is that she isn't. And yet, despite time and distance having parted us, I know so much more than she reveals. Like the expensive dresses she wears, the illusion of Martha is a facade, an elaborately constructed costume that she wears to cover up a pain she can in no other way conceal. I wonder now why, after all this time, she is still so scared to let her true self show.

I tap at the door and she spins at the sound.

'You made me jump,' she says, something aloof in her tone. She has been looking at me differently all evening, I've noticed, barely bothering to talk to me and only doing so when necessary. I have upset her somehow, or upset one of the others, though I've no idea what I'm supposed to have done.

She reaches for her robe where it lies on the bed, putting it on and pulling it tightly around herself, suddenly self-conscious.

'I'm sorry.'

She waits for more. 'Was there something you wanted?'

'I get the feeling I've done something to upset you. Holly too. I'm sorry... I don't know what it is.'

She deliberates over something she's tempted to say, apparently deciding to keep it to herself; for now, at least.

'You're lying to Holly, aren't you? I can't work you out, but I know you're not telling her the truth.'

'My friendship with Holly is nothing to do with you, Martha,' I tell her. 'And why are *you* lying to her?'

Her eyes narrow, and yet despite how hard she looks, she still doesn't see. 'What do you mean?'

'You're not being honest about who you are either, are you?'

She laughs nervously, a sharp exhalation of breath that betrays her defiant body language. 'I don't know what you're talking about. You don't know me. We've only just met.'

'I know you're lying to yourself. You've been lying to yourself your whole life.'

She looks angry, prepared for retaliation, but there is a flicker of her irises, enough to reveal that she's unsettled by my words.

She steps closer. Her perfume is beautiful, expensive and subtle. Intoxicating. 'You seem to have something you want to say to me,' she says softly, keeping her voice almost to a whisper, trying to intimidate me with her calmness. 'So just say it.' This isn't her; I know it even after all this time. She wants to present an image of herself as hard-shelled and impenetrable, but this isn't who she really is. I have followed her through Holly, hearing stories, seeing photographs online, watching her mature from a teenage girl into a woman, and I have seen for myself the persona she portrays to the world. It must be tiring for her, all this acting. So many times I've wondered whether she longs for someone with whom she can drop the performance.

I move a hand to her bare arm, testing her reaction. I expect her to swipe it away, still in denial, yet she doesn't.

'You don't remember me, do you? Perhaps if I had introduced myself as Annie, would you have remembered me then?'

She tries to hide her reaction, but it cannot be concealed. A brief shake of the head, nothing more, but enough to show that everything she might have thought about me until this moment has now been proven a lie. The name has been instantly recognised. She remembers everything.

'No,' she says, not wanting to believe, perhaps, that she has missed what has been right in front of her. 'You?'

I nod.

She sits on the edge of the bed, her face pale with disbelief. 'You look so different. I mean, I thought you seemed familiar, but I would never have known it was you.'

'It's been almost twenty years.' And there are other things too, I think; there are reasons for the difference in my appearance. I have lost a lot of weight, some through trying, then through treatment. Time has changed me. Yet I say nothing more.

'But you knew me.'

'Time has obviously been kinder to you.'

I sit beside her. She is so close that I could reach for her hand, but I don't allow myself to do it. It's safer with the space between us.

'You never contacted me,' I tell her, trying to hide the crack in my voice that splinters my words. Even after all this time, the pain of what happened between us is still there, as raw as though it was just yesterday.

'I couldn't. They were looking for you. The police. I could have told them about you, but I didn't.'

She tilts her head back and closes her eyes, losing herself for a moment to the details of the past. I have been back there too, so many times between then and now. I have lived a thousand versions, willing my memory into a series of falsehoods, but every time I have ended up at the same place, alone with what happened.

'A young woman in her early twenties,' she says. 'Brunette. I knew straight away it was you. No one else was able to identify you, so I knew it had to be you. Why were you even with him that night?'

'I wanted to make you jealous,' I tell her. 'You'd invited me there, but then it was like you regretted doing it. You did regret it, didn't you? You didn't want me there. So why did you ask me?'

'I was confused. I didn't know what I wanted.'

'And do you now, Martha? You're nearly forty years old, and you're still confused. Who are you trying to please?'

'No one. I'm not confused.'

But even she doesn't believe her words.

She does what I least expect her to and leans towards me, reaching for my face, pushing my hair gently back behind my ear. Then her focus moves from my eyes to my mouth, resting there for a moment before she moves her lips to mine. I have waited almost twenty years to kiss her again. She tastes exactly as she did the first time, expensive perfume and alcohol, her lips as soft as butter. Her fingers move from my face to my throat, their tips smooth and cold against my skin.

'I didn't stop thinking about you.'

And somehow her words make it worse. Had she regretted meeting me – had she wished she had never invited me to the party that evening – I could accept that everything that followed was fate, a naturally occurring cycle of inescapable events. Rejection is inevitable; a rite of passage. Yet none of that is true. She didn't reject me, not in the traditional sense. We have both longed for one another all these years, both caught in the memory of the other person; things might have been so different if only we had been braver, if only we had made different choices. If only we had been different.

Martha moves her hand from my face. 'What happened with Joseph? What did you do?'

'Ask me what he did,' I say. 'I'll tell you everything, I promise.'

NINETEEN

Holly

Caleb pushes me back through the door of the steam room. He is soaking wet, his dark hair plastered to his forehead, the beanie hat he was wearing not so long ago now abandoned somewhere. His arm is bleeding, a wide incision sliced into his skin.

'I thought you were an intruder!' I reach for his arm with a hand that trembles, sick with the thought that I have injured my son. Ruby-red blood swells to the surface of the wound in a dark bubble, trickling across the hairs of his forearm. 'That needs stitches.'

He yanks his arm away from me as I choke on tears. What sort of mother am I? I didn't even recognise my own son. What is he doing here?

'It's fine,' he says, though we can both see that it's not.

'Who's in there with you?' I demand, realising the stupidity of the question. Georgia. Why else would he be here? Is this why she was crying in the car, and why Toni refused to leave her? Perhaps Martha was right all along. Some boy had dumped her. I just never dreamed for a minute that the boy would be my son.

'Christ, Caleb... no. She's like a sister to you.'

There's less than eighteen months between Georgia and Caleb, and as Toni and I were the best support that either of us had in coming to terms with being young single mothers – a title that caused untold stigma for both of us in varying ways – our children grew up together like siblings. As toddlers they loved and fought with each other in equal measure, best friends and mortal enemies. The thought of them together is wrong. I imagine that, like me, Toni had no idea that anything had been going on between them. And now it occurs to me that perhaps she still doesn't know.

I bang on the door, wondering what sort of state of dress – or undress – Georgia is in. I presume she has a bikini on, though it occurs to me that she may be in there naked. 'Georgia. Come out here now, or I'll go and get your mother. Do you want her to see you like this?'

She moves behind the door, silhouetted for a moment in the frosted glass. I try to ready myself for the lecture I am about to deliver, but when the door opens, I realise there was nothing that might have prepared me for what I find.

Zoe stands in front of me, her skin glistening wet, a gold string bikini barely covering her. 'Holly,' she says quietly, eyes pleading with mine.

'No. No, no.' I laugh a humourless laugh, bitterness ringing on its echo. 'This is a joke, isn't it?' I look to Caleb. 'Tell me this isn't happening.'

'Holly, let me explain.' She reaches for my arm and I hit it aside.

'Shut up.' I step back from them, trying to make sense of everything. Claire's words. Her accusation. I have no idea how she made a connection between Zoe and Aaron, but perhaps she saw a series of dots and joined them together in the wrong sequence. Not Aaron, but Caleb.

'You can't explain anything,' I say to her, my voice brittle. 'What the hell were you thinking, Zoe? He's a child, for God's sake!'

'He's nineteen. He's not a child.'

'He's my child,' I snap, my voice breaking, on the verge of tears. 'And you're supposed to be a friend.'

She is right, I know: Caleb is no longer a child. I didn't recognise him as my own son less than ten minutes ago, believing him to be a grown man. But of course that's what he is. He is free to make his own choices and his own mistakes. But not like this. Not with her.

'What the hell are you doing here?' I ask him.

'I needed to see her.'

'For what? For this?' I'm unable to keep the disgust from my voice. 'It couldn't wait until Monday, could it? You had to sabotage your own mother's hen weekend.' I put a hand to my head as I walk away from them, feeling the strain of a headache pounding at my temples. 'This is sick, you know that, don't you?'

When I turn back to them, Caleb has distanced himself from Zoe. He is looking at the tiled floor between his feet, his head hanging like a child caught somewhere he shouldn't be.

'Cover yourself up, for God's sake.' I grab the robe that Zoe has discarded on a sunlounger and throw it at her, and she dresses hastily without speaking. 'So what was so urgent that it couldn't wait?'

Caleb looks at Zoe and then to me before shaking his head. Whatever it is he came here to see her about, I don't think he has even told her yet. 'It can wait,' he mumbles.

'No, it can't fucking wait.'

I hear my voice, but it isn't me. In almost nineteen years, I don't think I have ever sworn at my son. I have been angry with him at times, frustrated, disappointed, but he has never stunned me in the way that he has done this evening. This isn't him. This isn't how he behaves.

'Mum, please. I can't.'

I walk away from them again, this time crossing the room to go to the bifold doors. Outside, the sky is a curtain of falling stars, the ground carpeted in thick snow. It is beautiful and eerie.

'How long have you been here, Caleb?'

'Not long. You know that, you just followed me.'

'I don't mean here, in this room,' I say angrily, striding back towards him. 'I mean how long have you been in the village?'

He can't have just recently arrived; it would have been impossible. Sean left hours ago, ending his time here early in case he got cut off by the weather. Within an hour of him leaving, the lanes would have been impassable. Caleb must have been here for hours already, if not longer.

'Did you stay here this morning to see him?' I turn on Zoe, her lies gathering speed as they come flooding back. 'Was that why you were late going to the pub?' When she says nothing, anger fuels my words. 'What was so urgent then, Caleb – I still don't think you've told either of us, have you? What happened this morning? Couldn't you find the right words? Or did you get distracted with other things?'

I look at Zoe, her wet hair clinging to her face, her cheeks flushed with heat, and I feel a sudden revulsion. I considered her a friend. 'How long have you been sleeping with my son?'

My words make her visibly cringe. 'Holly, please, it isn't—'

'Oh my God.' I press my fingertips to my eyes. 'Dean. This is what you were trying to tell me last night.'

Zoe starts crying. If she is looking for sympathy, she won't find it from me. I can't feel sorry for her, not when she has brought everything on herself. If she had told me last night, at least it would have meant that she had admitted to her wrongdoings, but letting me find out like this, during my own hen weekend, feels like a certain kind of betrayal, premeditated.

'I wanted to tell you,' she pleads, her voice pathetic. 'I've wanted to tell you for months.'

'Months?' But of course it's been going on for months. I already knew this, if I'd had a chance to process it. Zoe has been separated from Dean since last summer. 'All those conversations at work,' I remind her. 'All the support I offered you.'

'I know. I know, and I'm sorry, Holly, I really am. I was going to tell you.'

'Yeah? When?'

I turn away from them again, trying to figure out how their relationship could have possibly begun. Caleb is a registered patient at the surgery where Zoe and I work. Did they meet there? When I think of everything I've said to her over the past couple of months, all the reassurances I've delivered in an attempt to ease the pain I thought she was experiencing in the aftermath of her break-up, I feel even more angered by her betrayal, and sickened by my own naïvety. I have been an older-sister figure to her, supporting her in any way I could, while all the time she was meeting with my son, a teenager – still in so many ways just a boy – and then lying to my face. I wonder just how much they have laughed at me behind my back.

How on earth am I going to hide this from my friends? It is shameful and embarrassing, and despite everything he's done, I want to protect my son. He is young and he is stupid, and I will always feel this instinctive need to keep him safe from the judgement of others. Zoe is the person I am truly angry with.

'You need to go and distract everyone,' I say.

She looks at me incredulously. 'What? How?'

'I don't know, Zoe, think of something. You're an imaginative liar, you'll work it out. Just don't mention Caleb to anyone, all right? No one can know he's here. Tell them I've been sick and I want to be left alone.'

Caleb is still looking at the floor between his feet, a reprimanded child awaiting punishment. He looks pathetic somehow, misplaced.

'Where's the car?'

'Just down the lane. There's a passing point about a mile away, I left it there.'

At least none of the others will see it, I think. I'm going to have to keep Caleb hidden here somehow; he can't drive back now, not with conditions as they are, but I don't want anyone else finding out that he's here. The shame of it is more than I think I can stand. My colleague and my son, shagging in the steam room at my hen weekend. I can't imagine a way in which things could be more humiliating.

He must have been here for hours already, the house big enough that he has managed to avoid bumping into me or any of the others.

How could Zoe do this to me? How could *he* do this to me?

'Distract them in the living room for as long as you can,' I tell her. 'Make sure no one goes into the kitchen.'

We wait in silence when Zoe leaves. Caleb tries to instigate conversation, but every time he speaks, I prompt him back to silence. I can't bear to look at him or talk to him.

'Come on,' I say eventually.

We make our way down the passage that leads to the kitchen. There is no one here. I wait at the kitchen doorway, listening for the sound of voices and laughter coming from the living room. The others must be wondering where I am, but whatever distraction Zoe has found, it is sufficient to keep everyone gathered in one place.

I usher Caleb through to the hallway and he follows me up the stairs. It won't be long before one of them wants to check on me to see how I am, and I need to get back downstairs before that happens. I'm going to tell them that it wouldn't be fair on Suzanne to make her sleep in the same room as me tonight. I'll ask Martha if she can join her. They seem to be getting on well, so I doubt either of them will mind.

We get up to the bedroom and I close the door behind us. 'You stay in here.'

'For how long?' he asks, pouting at the inconvenience despite the fact that he caused it himself.

'However long it is before you're able to drive home.' When he opens his mouth to object, I immediately shut him down. 'You made the choice to come here, Caleb. These are the consequences.'

He sits on the edge of the bed and rests his elbows on his knees. He looks suddenly younger again. Vulnerable. 'I've fucked up, Mum.'

'No shit.' I sit next to him. 'Why does Zoe think you came here?'

'To see her. I don't know, it felt dangerous. Exciting, I suppose.'

I fight off my reaction, holding back what I want to say. 'So why did you really come?'

'To warn her, but I haven't done it yet. Georgia knows about us. I think she's come here to hurt Zoe.'

TWENTY

Suzanne

Martha and I met two weeks before the house party, at a cinema complex on the outskirts of Longwell Green. I had gone there with someone from college to see *Gothika*; an awkward friendship that had been forced by our respective isolation from the rest of the girls in our year group. I despised scary films, but when she suggested it, I accepted the offer, for little reason other than to piss off my mother. I wanted her to see that I could stand on my own two feet. I wanted her to believe that there were people who liked me, who wanted to spend time with me. I wanted her to realise that the hold she had over me wouldn't last forever.

If only I had known what was to come.

After the film had ended and we got back to my friend's car, we realised we didn't have enough change between us to pay for the parking ticket. She was standing behind us in the queue: a tall, flame-haired girl with the prettiest eyes I had ever seen. She caught me looking at her as my friend grappled with the machine, trying to retrieve a twenty-pence piece that had been swallowed up, never to be seen again, and when her eyes met mine, I felt something I had never felt before, the kind of electric spark I had read about in stories but had never believed was real.

'Here,' she said, rifling in her purse before passing my friend a collection of coins. 'Have this.'

Even her voice was beautiful, some smoky quality about it, mature beyond her years. While my friend thanked her and pushed the coins one by one into the ticket machine, Martha busied herself with her bag again. Without a single word being spoken between us, she had sensed the same as I had, some instant connection, and when she passed me a receipt with her name and number written on the back of it – in black eyeliner in the absence of a pen – I wondered at how someone so young could be so self-assured. After my friend had dropped me home, I found myself unable to stop thinking about the girl with the red hair. She became a fantasy. An obsession.

'I only went to that party to see you, you know that,' I tell her now. 'I would never have known about it if you hadn't invited me. Why *did* you invite me?'

For days after we met, I wondered whether the number was a fake; perhaps someone else's number, some cruel joke for which either I or the person who'd answer the call was the intended recipient. It was naïve of me to hope for even a moment that someone would show an interest that instant and instinctive in me. Nonetheless I sprayed the receipt with hairspray, fearing that the number might be smudged and wanting to preserve the possibility it presented. And then I called her.

'I wanted to see you,' she says.

'But once I was there, what changed? You were so cold. It was humiliating.'

'I was confused. I wasn't in a good place; you know why.'

She told me about the fire. During the conversations between that first meeting and the party, she confided in me more than anyone else ever had, trusting me with secrets that seemed too personal for her to be sharing with someone who was little more than a stranger.

'So what was I, Martha? Collateral damage while you tried to "find yourself"?'

'It wasn't like that.'

'It felt like it.'

I had known from a young age that I was attracted to girls. While my classmates had bedroom walls adorned with posters of floppy-haired boy-band members, I was always more interested in the female presenters on Saturday-morning kids' television. I had been raised to believe that anything different was a threat, so when I realised that I was not like everyone else, for a long time I believed that I *was* the threat. Perhaps I was a threat to myself; or even worse, a threat to other people. I spent most of my young years avoiding socialising, getting lost in my own head, isolated with my secret. I had no one to tell; there was no one I could confide in. My mother would have disowned me had she found out, and I had no close friends at school to talk to about it.

Martha sighs, her eyes glassy and beautiful. 'I wanted to see you, but once you were there, I realised I just couldn't. There were too many people who—' She stops abruptly, not wanting to admit to the real reason why she shunned me that night.

'People? Or person?'

She holds my gaze and says nothing, but the look gives me her answer without her needing to speak the words. I know what it is like to suppress myself for a parent whose expectations are suffocating, to feel indebted to someone who has exerted such control over my life. Yet it was my own fault, to an extent, I know that now. I have known it for some time, despite never wanting to admit it to myself. I wonder what the hold was for Martha. Was it the guilt that after her mother and brother's deaths she was the only person her father had? Or was it financial dependence? Perhaps she feared being cut off from her father's business if he found out the truth of her sexuality. These are questions only she can answer, but I don't think she has even told herself the truth yet.

'You can't keep living a lie, Martha. You deserve to be happy.'

'Do I, though?'

'Why do you say that?'

There's an uncomfortable pause. 'I protected you,' she says, leaning forward conspiratorially, as though someone might be listening at the door. 'I didn't lie, but it was as good as a lie, wasn't it?'

'I know. And I'm grateful to you for that. I've always felt indebted to you.'

My admission throws us into silence. I wonder whether she will do anything with it, try to use it in some way to her own advantage. The truth is, I owe her my life. And I would gladly have given it to her.

'Why were the police looking for you? They said Joseph had been seen arguing with a young brunette. Why were you even with him? You didn't know him.'

I sigh, hating having to return to the memory. I was young and foolish, naïve – but none of these things are an excuse for what happened afterwards.

'I was trying to make you jealous. You'd hurt me, I was trying to hurt you back. It was a stupid knee-jerk reaction, I realised that afterwards. My pride had been hurt. I know we'd only just met, but I felt as though you understood me somehow. There was a connection. No one else had ever understood me, Martha. I needed someone who knew what it was like.'

She looks away, unable to meet my eye. She knows that what she did that night was wrong, inviting me there just to leave me feeling humiliated. I knew no one at the party, and I was all alone.

'I thought that if you saw me with a boy, it might make it even worse. It sounds cruel now, I suppose. It *was* cruel. But what you did was pretty cruel too.'

Her eyes meet mine, and I imagine that in this moment, she feels the same as I do. We are young again. I wish so very much that it could be true.

'I'm sorry.'

I wave a hand, dismissing the apology. 'You don't need to say that now. I'm just trying to explain what happened. Why I was talking to him. He was trying to make someone jealous as well – I realised that afterwards. We were using each other. I didn't really think too much of it at the time; I was too busy focusing on doing the same.'

'I didn't mean to hurt you,' Martha says. 'I was a mess back then... everything was so confused.'

I know she is referring to much more than her sexuality. I read up on the accident that killed her mother and brother. It had only happened a few years before we met, though something that like doesn't fade with time in the way that people are so often promised. I wondered then whether her father knew she was gay. I knew nothing of him, whether he was old-fashioned or whether he would have accepted her no matter what, but I learned enough to know that he was all she had, and I understood the pressure to please the very person who was preventing her from being her, if that was the case.

'I still don't understand,' she says. 'Joseph...'

'I flirted with him,' I admit. 'It was childish and stupid, I realised that afterwards.' I laugh bitterly. 'I realised a lot of things afterwards. All too late. I led him on, I suppose. I just wanted you to see me being noticed by someone else. I wanted you to feel that you'd made a mistake.'

'You *were* the girl who was mentioned in the press reports, weren't you?'

I have known for all these years that Martha protected me. She must have known when she saw the newspaper headlines and heard the reports on the local news that the young woman – 'late teens/early twenties, slim, brunette' – was me. No one else at the party had been able to identify me; no one who was able to name me came forward. I wasn't from the area, and there was only one person at the party that night who knew my name – a shortened version, no surname ever given. The person who had invited me there: Martha.

'You were seen arguing. What were you arguing about?'

I can't do it. So many times I have imagined how it might feel to be able to unload the truth of that evening after all these years, but now that the opportunity is here, the words are stuck in my throat.

Arguing. That was how it was witnessed by whoever had seen us together. In the dark, with a view distorted by alcohol and God knows what else, someone had interpreted it as some sort of lovers' tiff.

'I don't want to talk about it now,' I tell her, my chest tightening at the memory.

'So when?' she urges. 'I've got a right to know what happened, haven't I? I withheld evidence for you. I could have got into serious trouble if the police had found out I wasn't telling the truth. Something in my gut told me you had nothing to do with his death. Or was I wrong? What the hell did Joseph do?'

'It was my fault. I led him on.'

Martha pulls a face as she tries to put the pieces together, forming a mental jigsaw of all the things that have been left unsaid. Something behind her eyes changes as the realisation settles upon her.

'Hang on. You said that Joseph was trying to make someone

jealous? But Holly wasn't there – not for long, anyway. They argued and she went home. It's one of the things that's always cut her up about that night, that their last words were spoken in anger.'

'It wasn't her fault,' I say. I am grateful that her thoughts have been sidetracked, the focus moved for a moment from what happened in those moments that changed everything.

Martha stands and goes to the window, presses her palms to the sill, trying to expel the tension from her body. 'If Holly wasn't there,' she says, turning to me, 'then who was Joseph trying to make jealous?'

'I don't know.'

She shakes her head. 'No. You said he was trying to make someone jealous. You would only have known that if you'd seen it. Who was it?'

'Why is that important?' I stand too and go to her. 'It was almost two decades ago. My memories of that night are as distorted now as yours probably are. The details don't matter.'

'Of course they matter! Joseph died, and no one ever really found out why.'

'It was an accident, Martha. Sometimes there is no "why". Things just happen.'

We are interrupted by a knock at the door. Martha opens it; Zoe is outside. 'What?' she says, too abruptly.

'I'm just gathering everyone in the living room.'

'What for?'

'I'll show you when you get there.' She pokes her head around the door. 'Come on. We're all here for Holly, remember?'

Martha pulls a face, unimpressed by Zoe's unnecessary reminder.

'Some of us remember that, yes,' she says curtly, and she gives Zoe a look that's so cutting it makes me wonder what has happened between them.

She pulls her robe on over her nightdress and I follow her out onto the landing, knowing that our conversation is far from over. With Zoe ahead of us, Martha pauses at the top of the stairs, waiting for me to catch up with her. Her hand slips into mine, and she squeezes my fingers gently before letting go.

TWENTY-ONE

Claire

We are all gathered in the living room, despite Holly's absence. Toni looks ready for bed, while Georgia sits beside her with an expression that says she would rather extract her own teeth for entertainment than have to be here a moment longer. She eyes Zoe with contempt, presumably resentful at being coerced here with whatever promise of excitement that has been offered. I'm still not sure what we're doing here. All I can be sure of at this moment is that my head hurts, I feel as though I might throw up, and I regret too much of today. The room is making me dizzy, as though the floor might be pulled from underneath me at any moment. I just want to go home now, for this all to be over.

'Holly's been sick,' Zoe explains, casting me a reproachful look, as though it is somehow my fault. 'She said she needs a bit of time to herself. I thought I could entertain us for a while until the party gets restarted.'

'I think the party's over,' Martha says flatly.

'Did it get started then?' Georgia picks at a fingernail as she studies Zoe contemptuously. 'I hadn't noticed.'

'Georgia,' Toni says, though her tone holds no conviction. She doesn't sound like a mother who is able to take charge of her daughter's behaviour; if anything, she sounds brow-beaten by her, accepting that this is the way that Georgia is. It was this same lameness in her daughter's younger years that's allowed her to become what she is now: sullen, rude, obnoxious.

'You've been upstairs since we got here,' Martha responds with a forced smile. 'You wouldn't have noticed anything, would you?'

Georgia opens her mouth to say something, but Suzanne gets there first. 'We've all had a bit to drink, we're all tired. Zoe, what have you got for us?'

'A quiz,' she says, and several of us groan at the prospect. 'I mean, it's a bit impromptu, so I'm not that prepared, but it'll be fun.'

'Yay.' Georgia again, trying as much as she is able now to stir things up. Her head twitches as she eyes Zoe spitefully, her lip curling into a sneer. Her whole manner is twitchy and on edge, and despite being seated, she can't stay still. I wonder whether she's been drinking. Surely Toni would have said something to try to stop her?

'Okay, let's split into teams,' Zoe says, her enthusiasm starting to look a bit misplaced considering how quiet she's been all day.

'I preferred her when she was doing her disappearing act,' Martha mumbles, shuffling along the sofa to allow me to sit beside her and Suzanne.

'Fuck this shit.' Georgia gets up and heads to the door, but Zoe steps in front of her, blocking her path. For an uncomfortable moment, it looks as though Georgia might hit her. Her right hand is clenched into a fist at her side, and Zoe senses it before seeing it, her body flinching as she braces herself for the attack.

'Get out of my way,' Georgia says, her flushed face too close to Zoe's. She *must* have been drinking, I think. The red cheeks, the attitude, the sudden flare of anger. I wonder why it has so far been directed at Zoe, particularly as it's Martha who's given her reason to react.

Then, through the haze of alcohol that clouds my brain, an idea drops like a stone. Does Georgia know about Zoe and Aaron? But why would she care?

'We need you,' Zoe tries to reason, her voice wobbling. 'Even numbers.'

'It's not, though, is it?' Georgia says, mocking Zoe's now-departed too-cheerful tone. 'You're doing the questions, so you don't count. That makes five of us. If I leave, that evens the teams. Maths not your strong point at school? How long ago was school for you, Zoe?'

The atmosphere has become tense and strange, nobody sure why Georgia has adopted a sudden attitude towards Zoe. Suzanne casts me a questioning expression, which I can only respond to with a shrug. Toni stands and goes to her daughter, putting a hand on her arm to pull her away. 'Stop it, Georgia, this isn't like you,' she says, as though Georgia is five years old and is showing off to the grown-ups.

'How would you know what's like me and what's not, Mother? You don't know the first thing about me really, do you?'

There is something wrong with Georgia; her behaviour is erratic. She is shifting from foot to foot, her arms twitching at her sides as though she's developed a nervous tic. Toni is pushed too far this time; she grips her daughter by the arm and pulls her towards the living room door, despite Zoe's efforts to keep them in here.

'Let's all calm down, shall we?' Zoe suggests, but without conviction. She moves again, blocking the doorway. I look at

Martha and Suzanne, whose faces in the moment seem a mirror of each other's, reflecting the thoughts of everyone in the room. What the hell is going on?

'Just let her deal with her daughter, Zoe, for God's sake,' Martha snaps.

Toni is still holding Georgia by the arm, but she is shoved aside as the girl's temper finally spills beyond her control. 'Get your hands off me!'

Georgia pushes Toni, harder than I suspect she meant to. Toni stumbles back, shocked by her daughter's violence, but before anyone is able to react, Georgia turns her anger on Zoe again.

'Why are you here?' she says, her words a hiss in Zoe's face.

'Georgia—'

'Fuck off, Martha, it's nothing to do with you.' She returns her focus to Zoe. 'What are you doing here? You're not Holly's friend. Does she know what you've been up to yet?'

Zoe holds Georgia's stare, but her resolve is weakened and she looks like she might burst into tears.

'Georgia,' Toni says. 'This is Holly's hen weekend. Don't spoil it for her, please.'

'I'm not the one spoiling it! Ask this two-faced bitch who's really doing that.'

And now everyone wants answers from Zoe. Her face has turned scarlet, her cheeks flaring. She looks to me for support, but I'm the wrong person; she won't find any sympathy from me. Somehow Georgia also knows Zoe's secret. Her anger suggests only one thing; why else would she be so upset by the affair? The idea that Georgia is carrying Aaron's baby makes me feel sick, the champagne in my stomach churning, threatening to surge. Beside her, Toni is oblivious to what has been going on, her face a confusion of unanswered questions.

'I don't believe this,' Martha mutters, glaring at Zoe.

'I'm going to bed,' Zoe says. She steps around Georgia to

leave the room, but Georgia grabs her by the hair and yanks her back. Before anyone is able to stop her, she lands a swift and vicious punch to Zoe's left eye. Zoe falls back, disorientated, her eye encircled in an instant angry red mark.

Screaming ensues as Toni grabs her daughter and pulls her out into the hallway. One of us should get up to see to Zoe, yet none of us moves.

'Are you okay?' Suzanne asks.

In the hallway, Toni and Georgia are arguing.

'I'm fine.'

Zoe wants to leave, but she can't without having to go past Georgia and Toni. We wait and listen as the argument moves away from us, shifting upstairs; only then does Zoe go, leaving the rest of us sitting in silence.

'That wasn't normal,' Martha says. 'Georgia's acting like she's taken something.' Her mouth twists with anger and she stands suddenly, knocking her leg against the coffee table. 'What a fuck-up. I'm going to go and see if Holly's okay.'

'I'll go,' I say quickly.

Martha rolls her eyes. 'Whatever, Claire.' She looks at Suzanne. 'Shall we go up to bed?' She addresses her as though they are an elderly married couple, and Suzanne follows like an obedient pet, her apparent new best friend.

I don't want Martha to speak to Holly before I do. She doesn't know what's going on. She may have misinterpreted things, and she didn't see Zoe getting out of Aaron's car this morning. I don't want to have to do what I'm about to, but I know it will be better coming from me.

Before going upstairs, I head to the kitchen and get a glass of water. I take it up to Holly's room and tap gently at the door, waiting for her to answer. She has been crying.

'Are you feeling any better?' I ask, handing her the water.

'A bit,' she says. She smiles, but there is nothing real behind it. 'Too much champagne.'

'Can I come in?'

She glances behind her. 'I'm in a bit of a mess. I need to clean up.'

'I can help you, I don't mind.'

'No,' she says abruptly. 'Really, it's fine. Thanks, though.'

'Where's Suzanne?'

'I asked her if she'd mind sharing with Martha tonight. Not nice for her to be stuck in here with me if I'm sick again. I—'

'Hol—'

We speak over one another, cutting each other short.

'Go on.'

'There was an incident downstairs,' I explain. 'Between Zoe and Georgia.'

'I did hear something.' I notice that she doesn't seem surprised by the news. If anything, it appears that she might have been expecting it.

'What I said earlier, about Zoe not being a friend—'

'I know, Claire.'

For a moment I am unsure what she means – that she knows Zoe isn't a friend, or that she knows about the affair with Aaron. Perhaps all she means by it is that she knows the comment was made. She surely can't know that Georgia is involved in any of this, so I wonder what she presumes their argument was about. 'You know what?' I ask.

'I don't want to talk about it.'

'I just—'

'Claire, I'm tired and I don't feel well. Please, can we just leave this for now?'

Holly is nothing like herself. Has she already spoken to Zoe? If she has, it has changed her. She seems a different person to the woman she was little over an hour ago. She closes the door on me without a further word, as though I am in some way to blame for what Zoe has been doing behind her back. Yet even with the raging headache that pulses at my temples and presses at the front of my brain, I know that I am a hypocrite. Amid all the mess that today has become, one thought prevails: I am no better than Zoe, not really. I have lied, I have cheated, I have carried my own secrets.

And at times, like now, it feels as though those secrets might kill me.

TWENTY-TWO

Holly

With everyone in bed, I stalk the landing, paranoia having settled in my gut like an infection. Caleb is still in my bedroom, already complaining about the boredom; to my knowledge, no one else other than Zoe knows he is here. I'm pretty sure Claire didn't see anything when she came to my room, and she probably believes that my behaviour is down to supposedly knowing about Zoe and Aaron. I am hoping that the snow will thaw by morning and that it will be safe for Caleb to leave before anyone realises he is here, although it's so cold tonight, I doubt that will happen. The snow's too deep already, though it may not be so bad further along the lane where he has left the car.

I asked him where Aaron thinks he's gone; Caleb told him he was going to stay at a friend's house for the night. He asked if he could borrow the car so that they could go to one of the bigger skate parks at the other side of Bristol, and unsuspecting Aaron must have said yes without question. He had no plans to go anywhere this weekend, and was probably looking forward to having the house to himself, but his trust in Caleb is something I'm unsure whether I should be grateful for or disappointed in.

Finding out that Caleb has been having sex with Zoe has left me feeling sickened, yet the knowledge that he has also been seeing Georgia leaves me feeling even worse. After telling me he thinks Georgia has come here this weekend to hurt Zoe, Caleb admitted that he has been seeing both women for a while. Toni is one of my closest friends, and she cannot have known what was going on between him and Georgia. If she had, I'm pretty sure she would have told me. What were they thinking, crossing boundaries like that? As far as I can remember, they've never shown any interest in each other in that way, or perhaps they were just clever enough to keep it hidden from us. I didn't raise my son to become this person, but perhaps I don't know him as well as I thought I did.

Pacing the floor does nothing to help my nerves, so I stop by a radiator, trying to melt the iciness that sits within me, embedded in my chest since finding Caleb with Zoe in the steam room. Am I overreacting? Have I not reacted enough? Everything I think and feel has become exaggerated, driven by an unknown force. I have no control in steering my own emotions, and I'm scared where they will lead me. And then there is the still unresolved issue of Suzanne.

If I had known this afternoon that the day would lead to all this, I would never have started drinking. I need a clear head, but there is no chance of that now. And how could I have possibly anticipated that this was where my hen weekend would take me?

I still wonder how Claire made a link between Zoe and Aaron. It wouldn't have come from Georgia, I know that much, because I'm sure that Toni has no idea what's been going on between her and Caleb. I might have been able to talk about it to Claire had she not drunk so much, but the combination of champagne and the medication mean that she's in no fit state to be relied upon for advice. Besides, there's nothing that anyone can do now. The damage is done.

I should have stuck with the four of us this weekend: me, Claire, Martha and Toni. My oldest friends. The ones I can rely on. I felt sorry for Zoe, thinking a weekend away would do her good, help her to take her mind off things; and as for Suzanne, well, Suzanne and I share a history. I thought we understood each other. Now, I don't know what to believe is true and what's not. They have both proven themselves not to be real friends at all, and I regret having invited them. I know that without them here, I wouldn't be feeling the way I am now. I don't think I've been difficult about anything in the build-up to this wedding – in fact, I've asked for nothing, careful not to put pressure on anyone, financially or otherwise – but I had at least expected that my hen party would be a fun and relaxing couple of days. A chance to catch up on everything that's been missed.

I suppose, in a way, that's exactly what is happening.

Suitably warmed, my pacing resumes. I feel my cheeks burn with humiliation at the thought of all the lies I have been told, all the secrets that have been kept hidden from me. Have they been laughing at me all this time, Suzanne and Zoe, revelling in their respective deceptions, mocking me for how stupid I must be not to have picked up on any of their lies? Kind, reliable Holly – what an idiot.

I should go to bed, but I can't bear to be in the same room as Caleb, and I know he won't be comfortable sharing a room with his mother. His problem. He shouldn't be here. He should never have let his dick rule his brain. I can't believe that I am having these thoughts about my own son.

At the end of the corridor, I stop at the sound of voices. Suzanne is staying in Martha's bedroom tonight, though I had thought they would be both be asleep by now. I move closer to the doorway, resting against the frame as their voices intensify.

'Please don't keep asking me. It's all so long ago now.' Suzanne's voice, hushed to little more than a whisper.

'I need to know,' Martha says. 'Secrets always come out in the end, one way or another.'

'But you've managed to keep yours for long enough.'

I push the door wide. 'What secrets?' I look from Martha to Suzanne and back again. Both women look guilty. What could Martha possibly have to look guilty about?

I don't need to fake the appearance of sickness, not when I must look green with anxiety. I have been so focused on Zoe and Caleb that I had abandoned all thoughts of the severity of Suzanne's lie, neglecting myself for a moment in the instinctive act of looking out for my son.

I've still not confronted Suzanne with my suspicions about her mother. There hasn't been a good moment to do it, not while we're stuck out here in this place with all the others. Whatever I say and whenever I say it, I am sure she will be prepared with yet another falsehood. After all, she's had almost two decades to construct her story.

'Cat got your tongues?'

Even to my own ears, my voice no longer sounds like mine. I am changed tonight, a different person to the one I was when we arrived here yesterday. A thought passes through me, unwanted but inescapable. What if all these women are toxic? What if I am surrounded by liars?

Don't allow yourself to think that, Holly, I tell myself. These are your closest, your best friends.

'What's so long ago?'

In all the years I have known her, I don't think I have ever seen Martha embarrassed. Until now. 'Holly—'

'We know each other,' Suzanne blurts. 'I mean, we already knew each other before this weekend. We met once before, years ago. I thought I recognised Martha yesterday, but it's only this evening that I've worked it out.'

Martha nods slightly but says nothing. I know they are lying; I can feel it in my gut, like the onset of a sickness bug, something niggling inside me, alerting me to the illness waiting there. Perhaps that's what all these women are. Parasites. Diseases.

'I spoke to your mother, Suzanne,' I tell her.

She looks flustered for a moment, but it is only brief. 'Did you? None of us has got any signal.'

I can't help but laugh; it is either that or cry. 'That's your first thought? Not the fact that she's supposed to be dead?'

Beside her on the bed, Martha looks down at her hands, shifting uncomfortably. Does she know? I wonder. But I cannot bring myself to dwell for too long on the possibility. Not Martha too.

'Did you want me to find out? I mean, you said something to Martha, didn't you? About people arguing with their mothers.'

No one speaks. No one, even now, has the decency to be honest with me.

'Your mother's not dead at all, is she?'

Suzanne, backed into a corner, has no choice but to admit to her lie. Not that she needs to say the words; they are written all over her face.

'Oh my God.' I sit in the chair at the end of the bed. I want to leave the room, leave this house, be anywhere but here, but with two feet of snow outside, there is no escaping this place, and there is now no escaping this truth. 'We met at a bereavement group,' I say, as though she needs reminding of the fact. I look her in the eye, this friend of so many years. This stranger. 'You were grieving your mother.'

She closes her eyes. Beside her, Martha's eyes meet mine, wide and glassy, begging for my forgiveness. 'I didn't know,' she tells me. 'I swear I didn't know about this.'

'I remember the first time you came to the session,' I say, ignoring Martha and concentrating my focus on Suzanne. 'You were so nervous. It was like you couldn't speak. When the woman running the place said something to you, your face went bright red. I felt sorry for you. You didn't want anyone to pay you attention, and I knew exactly how that felt. You wanted to disappear, and I got that. I'd spent those past couple of months wanting to disappear, wanting to die at times, but I couldn't. I had Caleb. He needed me.'

I swallow back a sob. I will not cry in front of this woman. A terrifying thought sweeps over me, one I haven't yet fully allowed myself to experience. I have no idea who she is. I don't know why she is in my life, when everything I thought I knew about her is a lie.

'We just connected, didn't we?' I say, unable to process the scale of her manipulation. 'Once you started talking, once you told me about your mother, it was like I'd finally found someone I could be honest with. Everyone else in my life was suffering along with me – I couldn't burden them with anything more than I already had done. It felt safe talking with you. But it was all a lie, wasn't it?'

Suzanne shakes her head. Until now, she has sat silently, shame keeping her words trapped inside her, but my accusation manages to rouse a response. 'Everything I told you about my mother was true.'

'Except the fact that she was fucking dead!'

I get up and go to the dressing table, fighting back the urge to pick up the nearest object and throw it across the room. In the mirror, my pale face stares back at me. My eyes are dark and sunken, less a bride-to-be and more a Hallowe'en ghoul confronting her own demons. I look nothing like me. What scares me more is that I no longer feel anything like me.

'Why did you join the bereavement group?' I ask, turning back to the room.

'I told you the truth about the kind of woman my mother was,' she says, not answering the question. 'The control, the manipulation, the way she'd always stifled me. Our relationship was exactly as I described it. I was always grieving her in a sense, grieving the life she took from me, grieving the mother I wish she had been.'

I laugh. There might be some humour to be found if it wasn't so tragically pathetic and nonsensical. There might be something to be amused by, somewhere, if the woman sitting in front of me – a woman I once considered a friend – wasn't a pathological liar. And this goes beyond lies. Only a psychopath could sustain this pretence for almost two decades.

'Poor Suzanne,' I say, sarcasm dripping from my words. 'I feel so sorry for you. So you joined a bereavement group because you didn't get the mother you wanted. Do you know how crazy that sounds?'

It hasn't occurred to me until now how adept she must be at telling lies. Liars get tripped up along the path of their storyline at some point, their string of untruths tangled, knotting in the confusion of what is remembered and what goes forgotten. A fork appears in the road, one way leading to the lie that has been told, the other to a truth that shouldn't need any rehearsal. The wrong path is chosen; the lie is exposed. Suzanne has been lying to me for years, never once contradicting herself or stumbling over some invented memory; or if she has, I was too blinded by her friendship to notice the error.

'So come on,' I say, turning my attention now to Martha. 'You haven't told me where you two met.'

'Don't, Holly,' Martha pleads, her voice frantic. 'Don't do this now.'

'When would you like me to do it?'

She sighs and closes her eyes, wishing herself away from this room as I have done. I don't want to hear what she's about to say, not when it already seems that once the shell of her words is opened, its contents might contaminate everything within its reach.

'Fuck,' I say quietly, trying to read her silence. 'Is anyone going to stop lying to me?'

She stands and moves around the bed. 'There's so much more than I can explain here and now. I promise you—'

'Where did you meet her?'

Martha's eyes widen. She looks so different suddenly, so unlike the woman I have known all these years. She is always so in control, so self-assured. But of course, she's not. It is all an act to hide the sadness she carries. Like Suzanne, Martha is an expert in wearing a carefully constructed facade. And it's this thought, that they may perhaps be so similar, that turns my blood to ice.

'In a car park,' Suzanne says. 'She gave me some change to pay for a parking ticket.'

I look from Martha to Suzanne and back again, wondering why a parking ticket is causing such secrecy. So many lies between them, lies between us, the truth waiting to explode in our faces.

'But that's not what you were talking about, is it? Just now, before I came in, you were saying something about secrets. What's the big secret, Martha?'

Martha looks to Suzanne as though she's requesting permission to speak, and the exchange makes me boil with anger. 'Will one of you just please tell me what the fuck is going on?'

'The party,' Suzanne says finally, the admission escaping on a whisper. 'I was there at the party the night Joseph died.'

NOW

SUNDAY

There is a wound on her head. From this angle, standing here, she can see it now. She fell, she remembers that. It is coming back in stages, slowly, details of the memory being drip-fed to her through a filter, her brain retaining the pieces it doesn't yet want her to recall.

She fell.

She hit her head.

There was blood.

She puts her hands either side of her own head, covering her ears, and staggers back, the swell of pain behind her eyes surging in a wave so powerful she feels it might drown her. They are looking at her, all of them, their eyes fixed upon her as though they know.

'Are you okay?' someone asks.

She puts a hand on the back of a sunlounger, steadying herself. Was this what she fell onto? Was this how she cut her head?

It wouldn't have killed her, she thinks. The lounger has a metal frame, but that alone wouldn't be enough to kill someone, would it? It was just a stumble, just a fall. It was just the frame of a sunlounger.

But there was blood.

She was on the floor.

There was blood coming from her ear.

She drops onto the lounger, her body weighted with grief and despair. God, she wishes she could remember. With her head back in her hands and her shoulders hunched forward, she begins to rock, the motion intensifying the feeling of sickness that was already racing through her. Think. Just think. You were here. You were with her. You know what happened.

But does she?

She was on the floor. She sees her then as vividly as she sees her now, her body in front of her, lifeless. Or not lifeless, just still.

She thought until now that she was guilty. That she killed her.

Now she realises that she didn't. She couldn't have. But if she was still alive when she left her, then what happened after she went? If she didn't kill her, someone else in this house did.

FOUR HOURS EARLIER

TWENTY-THREE

Suzanne

I didn't mean to hit Joseph. This is the first, most important fact about that night, and about everything else that followed. I didn't mean to hurt him. I didn't mean to kill him. I hadn't been drinking, but I had been crying, my vision blurred and distorted by a stream of tears that were expelled in both pain and anger – some for Joseph, more for Martha, most just for myself. Perhaps they were the real cause of the accident: if I hadn't been crying, I might have seen him there; I might have reacted differently, or quicker. I might have been driving slower. I wouldn't have panicked in the aftermath. He might still be alive now.

The party was in full swing, most of the teenagers there by now intoxicated on a heady mix of alcohol and freedom, but I couldn't stay a moment longer. I wanted to get away from him, and from her; I just wanted to be home, where I would be safe. My mother had always reminded me that it was the only place I could ever stay completely protected, by her side where she could look after me, and it seemed then that she had been right all along. For so long I had wanted to escape, but now that I had ventured further, freedom didn't look so appealing. The world was a scary and awful place, people capable of all kinds of horrors.

Capable of all manner of mistakes.

He was walking by a hedgerow. I didn't know that at the time; only afterwards, when I stopped the car. He had been tucked into the darkness, little more than an outline in the shadows. I was going too fast, I had known I was, but I didn't think too much of it at the time; the roads were quiet, there was only me there. I just wanted to get home. I felt a dull thud, and then there was silence. It happened so quickly, and yet the period between the impact and opening the car door seemed to stretch into its very own lifetime. When I finally got out of the car, my limbs were frozen by the possibilities of what I would find outside. An animal, I told myself, still trying desperately to convince myself that the worst thing imaginable had not just happened. A lost dog that had strayed too far from home; a fox blinded by the headlights.

I had to narrow my eyes to make him out; he was so much further from the car than I had thought he could be. The impact must have thrown him twenty feet. He was lying on his side, inert on the damp tarmac. It was too dark to make out the details, but I remember his eyes were shut, as though he was just sleeping. It took me a moment to realise that it was Joseph, my eyes struggling to adjust to the darkness. There must be a mistake, I thought. It couldn't be him. Not now... not after what had just happened.

But there was no mistake. He was wearing the same jacket I had seen him in earlier; I had been close enough to it then to recognise it instantly. I crouched beside him, blinded by tears as I spoke his name on an endless loop of panic, willing him to speak back to me, to say something, to just make a noise so that I would know he was okay. But there was nothing.

I waited, but there was nothing.

I drove away. In all the years that have passed between then and now, there hasn't been a single day when I've not thought about that moment in which the decision was made. I could have called someone for help; I could have run to the nearest house. But I didn't. I couldn't. If I had, the police would have asked too many questions. They would have found out that we had been to the same house party that evening; they would have spoken to the people who might have seen us both there. Someone might have seen what he did to me, out in the garden, and then no one would have believed that what had happened was an accident. I didn't mean to hurt him. But no one would believe that.

Instead of facing the questions and the consequences, I ran away. I drove home, the house shrunk in darkness when I got back; my life sucked within the confines of its four walls. I crept up the stairs, two at a time, anxious not to disturb my sleeping parents. I kept quiet and prayed that no one would be able to identify me from that night, knowing that there was one person who might mean the difference between prison and freedom. In spite of her rejection of me that evening, it was Martha who had an opportunity to save me, and when weeks passed and there was no knock at my mother's front door, I realised that she had. She had kept silent for me. She had rescued me.

Did she know what Joseph had done when he followed me into the garden? There were so many people there that night that it seemed to me that someone must have seen it – someone had; they had reported it to the police, referring to an 'argument' – and yet it was this very volume of people that made it then seem all the more impossible that it had been witnessed. It is easy to get lost in a crowd, and I was invisible – I had always been invisible – while he had been clever, the moment premeditated and meticulous, the corner of the garden offering a quiet space in which his almost-crime would go unnoticed.

And what had he done, really? In the eyes of the police, it would have been nothing. He didn't *do* anything.

This was the other reason I could never have gone to the police. I had flirted with him. I had done it openly, affronted by Martha's change in attitude towards me, my pride hurt by the way she had shunned me after making such a fuss about getting me to go to that party in the first place. We had been communicating by text and phone calls for weeks, getting to know one another, sharing secrets and desires. It had felt as though I had known her all my life, although I realised later that I had been blinded by the idea of her and by everything she represented. I had chosen Joseph at random, not realising that he was connected in any way to Martha or her friends. I stood close, I leaned in; I said things I knew were provocative, things I had never said to anyone before.

And then I noticed him looking at the other girl, watching her reaction to us, and I realised he was using me in the same way I was using him, trying to make someone else jealous.

I went into the garden for a cigarette. I was going to leave – there was no point in staying – but I wanted a smoke before I went back to the car, knowing I wouldn't be able to sneak out for one once I got back home. A boy came up to me when he saw the packet in my hand; he asked if he could have one. I lit it for him, grateful when he went somewhere else to smoke it. Then a hand touched my side. I thought it was someone else trying to cadge a freebie off me, so I held out the packet on autopilot, lacking the will to object.

It was Joseph. I smiled when I realised it was him, but the look went unreturned. Without speaking, he took the burning cigarette from my hand, took a drag and threw it on the ground before grinding it beneath his trainer.

'What are you doing?'

His hand flew to my mouth. He was so close I could smell the alcohol on his breath. He must have had far more to drink than I had realised when we were talking inside the house, and when he spoke, his words were slurred and angry. His palm covered my mouth, his fingertips pressed into my cheek. His left knee dug into my leg, pinning me against the wall of the shed.

'Do you still want it then?' he whispered in my ear.

I've tried to blank out what happened next, but even after nearly two decades, I can't. That moment returns to me like a recurring nightmare, the sounds and smells as alive as they were that night: the throb of bass from the house behind us, the lingering scent of tobacco that stained his fingers.

The hand that wasn't silencing me moved to my thigh, and when his fingers slid between my legs, I froze.

Then just as quickly as it had started, it stopped. He pulled away from me, assessing me as though I was an object in a shop window, something he'd contemplated buying but had changed his mind about. I tried to speak, but I was too shocked to form words, my vocabulary swallowed by fear. Then his expression changed, and I realised that he was just as scared as I was. Fearful of what he had done; frightened by what he might have been capable of doing. Scared now of how I might react.

Neither of us said a word, the stand-off broken when he left me there alone. He mumbled something, but I didn't make out what it was. Sometimes, in a memory I try to force from somewhere it doesn't really exist, I imagine it was 'slut'. Sometimes I remember it as 'sorry'. After he had gone, I stayed at the side of the shed, cold and trembling. Dirty. I hated myself. I wished I'd never gone there. I wished that I had never set eyes on Martha.

I had to go through the house to get to my car, managing to keep myself hidden between the groups of teenagers who lingered in the kitchen and the hallway. I was shaking as I fumbled in my bag for the keys, unable to control my hands as I tried to grip the steering wheel. The tears began as soon as I had pulled away from the kerb, the humiliation and the pain added to the blend of self-hatred I had already concocted for myself. The lane was just a few streets away, and that was when it happened. My life changed within those awful split seconds, and everything that would follow would come back to this night.

TWENTY-FOUR

Holly

There is too much to comprehend, and I don't know where to start in an attempt to make sense of Suzanne's words. She was at the party... why? She didn't live in the same town as the rest of us; she didn't go to the same college. None of us had ever met her before, though she met me afterwards. By chance? I can't believe that now. She lied to me about the death of her mother, continuing the pretence for almost twenty years. Why?

Why? Why? Why?

'I don't understand. You were there together?'

'I don't think we should do this now,' Martha says.

'Do what, exactly? Tell the truth?' I stand blocking the doorway, resolved to keep Martha inside the bedroom until the details of whatever secret they're hiding between them are brought out into the light. Whatever she was referring to when I was listening at the door, it has been kept from me for long enough. My focus moves between each of them in turn, and under my gaze they both seem to withdraw into themselves.

'Someone needs to speak.'

'I didn't realise who Suzanne was until an hour ago,' Martha tells me. 'I invited her to that party, after we met. We'd been chatting, and...'

'You fancied each other?' I say, finishing her sentence when she drifts into silence.

Why Martha has tried to keep her sexuality a secret all these years is a mystery to me, as it has always been to Claire and Toni. We all know that she's gay; we've known it since we were teenagers. There have been countless occasions on which she could have told any one of the three of us – there have been times we have orchestrated conversations in an attempt to make her feel comfortable enough to talk to us about it – yet she has always remained silent on the subject, never offering details of dates or partners, always managing to keep her love life separate from our friendship. It has been obvious for years that she knows we know, and so the four of us have danced around the subject. Less a secret, more something that for whatever reason Martha doesn't want to discuss.

'Yeah. We did.'

'So what happened?' I ask. 'At the party?'

Suzanne glances at Martha.

'I bottled it,' Martha admits. 'I asked Suzanne to come along, but once she was there, I backed out. I wasn't ready for people to know, you know?'

'We all knew,' I say. 'So not really.'

I sound cold. Heartless, even. Nothing like myself. As I stand here, I know that there is more: more I don't want to have to listen to but that I know I need to hear, because whatever this is about, it isn't about some teenage crush that led to nothing. I saw both their faces when I entered the room; I saw the guilt that flashed across Martha's eyes, and the panic that fixed upon

Suzanne's features. They are hiding something from me, and I need to know what it is.

'So you just went home?' I say to Suzanne. 'Did you see each other again?'

For the first time since I entered the bedroom, she meets my eye, and when she does, I realise I have no idea who I am looking at. Perhaps the same can be said for Martha, although I don't want to linger on the possibility that she has also been lying to me. It is one more person than I may be able to bear.

She shakes her head. 'I never saw Martha again after that night. Not in person, at least.'

Martha twitches at Suzanne's words.

'You mean you looked her up online?'

'Yes,' she says with a shrug, a casual admission to her internet interest in a woman she hasn't seen in almost two decades. She reacts as though it is normal. As though any of this is normal. The truth is, it is weird.

'I've mentioned Suzanne to you,' I say, turning my attention to Martha. 'Plenty of times. Did you never think it might be the same Suzanne? She must have seemed familiar to you in some way.'

'I introduced myself as Annie. That was the only name she knew me by.'

'So why the bereavement class? Why me?'

Martha and Suzanne – two of the women I have considered my closest friends for all these years – cannot bear to make eye contact with me. They can't bring themselves to look at each other either, eyes darting around, neither able to settle her focus upon any one point in the room.

'I shouldn't have done it, I realised that afterwards, but I just wanted to meet you. Then once we'd spoken, I felt a need to keep seeing you. We *did* understand each other. We had a connection. We still do, I truly believe that.'

'I don't understand you. You lied to me. You kept on lying. That's not a friendship, Suzanne.'

'Most of what I've told you is the truth. Everything I said about my mother, about the sort of relationship we had, that's all true. I did look after her through her illness – I still do.'

'But the basis of our relationship, the reason we started talking to each other in the first place... it's all a lie.'

Suzanne is shaking her head. Maybe she hopes to convince herself that she was justified in some way, or maybe she thinks her lies are true. 'I'm sorry. I'm so sorry, Holly, none of it should have ever happened. Once we started talking, I realised we had so much in common. We were good for each other. I never expected to feel the way I did towards you, but you made me feel better about myself. I was just curious at first. I needed to see you, to know that you were okay. To know that Caleb was okay. I wanted to make it up to you somehow. I thought that if I could just get close to you, I could help you—'

'Make what up to me?'

Martha's eyes have filled with tears. She is watching Suzanne with a concentration that is unsettling, and I realise suddenly that she knows what she is about to say. Whatever Suzanne is going to tell me, Martha knows. She has always known. And I don't want to hear it. I don't think I can bear to hear it.

And then it settles upon me, a truth so horrifying that I haven't allowed it until now to become so much as a possibility. The police were looking for her. She and Joseph had been seen arguing. The young woman who was never identified. The potential witness.

'No.' My vision blurs as I take a step backwards. 'No,' I say again, shaking my head. She doesn't speak. She doesn't need to tell me what happened that night, because I already know. 'Martha?' I say, appealing to her for help. Make it untrue, I want to plead with her. Please. Make it go away.

But Martha won't look at me. Suzanne stands up. 'I want to explain everything to you, Holly. Please.'

When she moves towards me, I take another step backwards, my hand held out to stop her coming any closer. 'Don't.'

'He did something to me, at the party. That's why I couldn't go to the police – they would never have believed it was an accident.'

'Shut up,' I tell her, the words escaping through gritted teeth.

'Holly, he followed me into the garden and—'

'Shut up!' I say again.

'I know you don't want to hear it,' Martha says, 'but she's telling the truth. I know you loved Joseph, but you put him on a pedestal, and he didn't always deserve to be there. We all knew he wasn't what you made him out to be, but you'd created this fairy tale for the two of you and no one was going to convince you otherwise.'

'She's a liar,' I spit, the words leaving me in a snarl. 'Haven't you just heard? She's been telling me for twenty years that her mother's dead when she's been alive all this time. You can't believe anything she says.'

'I saw it,' Martha says quietly.

Suzanne's head snaps towards her. Her eyes are wet with tears. 'Martha?'

'Sometimes we only see what we want to see,' Martha continues. 'You were besotted with him, Holly, we could all see that. I know you don't want to think anything bad of him now either, but—'

'Just stop it!' I scream.

Behind me, the bedroom door is flung open and Toni erupts into the room, wide-eyed and panicked. She is clutching a square of folded paper.

'Where's Claire?'

'What's happened?' I ask, grateful for the diversion from

Suzanne's revelations. I didn't hear the words; it isn't real. I didn't hear the words. It isn't real.

Toni bursts into tears. She thrusts the paper into my hand and the floor shifts a little further beneath my feet, everything I thought I knew to be true tipped off balance once again.

'What's this?'

'What does it look like?'

I put a hand on her arm and go with her onto the landing, leaving Martha and Suzanne alone in the bedroom. It is only now that I realise I am shaking.

'How could she do this?'

Toni's words float above me, lost amid the noise of my thoughts. *He did something to me.* Did what? Suzanne is a liar. I already know that everything that has left her mouth is a lie. She is a delusional fantasist, existing in a crazy world of make-believe she has designed for herself. I am nothing more than a puppet, naïve and exploited.

But the truth was there; I saw it in their eyes. Neither of them could bring themselves to say it. But neither of them needed to. The words were loud in the silence, written on both their faces. Suzanne was driving the car that killed Joseph.

TWENTY-FIVE

Claire

Zoe is in bed, her back turned to me. She is probably not asleep. She nursed her blackening eye with a damp towel earlier, but it didn't seem to help. I think she's milking the injury, portraying herself as the victim in the hope that it will take the focus off her. She barely spoke to me earlier, getting changed in the en suite and into bed without saying a word. I hope it is milder tonight, though I doubt there's much chance of that. If the snow hasn't started to thaw by tomorrow, I'm not sure how we're going to get home.

I don't want to be here any longer than we have to be. I want to get home to my boys, so I can begin to put things right.

When I check my phone, there is an email from one of my colleagues. I wonder what could be so important that she needs to contact me on a Saturday night.

You need to see this, she has written. *I'm sorry to have to do this, but my daughter saw it and recognised you. Make sure it gets taken down before someone from school sees it.*

There is an attachment. A photograph. When I open it, the room seems to stop as though frozen, everything that was blurred and spinning just moments ago now stilled into terrifying definition. It is too real, the image sharp and alive. I can't stop staring at it. It isn't me. It can't be me.

It is me. Me with Sean, the butler-in-the-buff who was here earlier today.

I zoom in on the screenshot, taking in the details of the social media page on which it has been posted. Instagram. Georgia. Over four hours ago. How many people might have seen it during that time? I scroll down the comments section, cringing at some of the cruel remarks that have been posted, all by teenagers who think they are immune from repercussions, free to say whatever enters their vicious little minds while behind the safety of their phone screens.

The state of it
Gran's ready for her dinner
Hahahaha! Sick
OMG, just brung up my breakfast
@liamo5 your mums been on the shots

'Claire.' Holly taps quietly at the door, taking my attention from my phone screen. She eases it open a little before I respond. I hide the phone beneath the duvet. I don't want her to know what Georgia has done, or for her to see that photograph. The fewer people who see it the better. I need to get it taken down.

She doesn't give me time to get out of bed; she is in the room and standing over me, her face pale and impassive as she asks me to go with her to Toni's room.

'What's happened?'

'Just come with me.'

I pull on the robe that Martha bought me, feeling the cold

take an instant bite at my skin. The alcohol should be warming me, but it seems to be having the opposite effect. I am ice inside, frozen to my core.

We reach Toni's room, but Holly stops outside, a hand resting on the handle. 'Is it true?' she asks.

'Is what true?'

She thrusts a piece of paper in front of me. My heart rolls in my chest at the sight of it, the air pulled from my lungs. The note in my bag. Someone went into my room and found it. It was stupid of me to bring it here. I should have disposed of it somehow before we arrived. I should have destroyed it after looking at it yesterday.

'Please just let me explain.'

'How can you explain this?' She looks as though she might cry, her eyes watery and tired. But there is something else, too: an anger that flares behind her focus, so uncharacteristic for Holly.

She opens the door. Toni is standing at the window, her arms folded across her chest and her eyes fixed upon a blank point on the wall. The whites of her eyes are glistening with tears, her dark make-up smudged at their corners, and I am sorry, so sorry; more sorry than either of them could ever realise. I didn't know what else to do. I was desperate. She cannot bring herself to look at me. I cannot bring myself to speak.

'God, Claire. I don't believe this.'

I wonder just how much Toni has told Holly: how many notes have been sent to her; how much money she has transferred to the anonymous PayPal account. In total, I have blackmailed her out of almost twenty-five thousand pounds. I needed the money to keep the house; it was the only way I was going to be able to raise that kind of cash. I did it for my boys. Everything I do, I do for my children. It has always been that way; it will always be that way.

'I'm sorry.'

The words are pathetic, empty. My head is screaming. I wish I hadn't drunk so much. I wish I hadn't taken that Xanax. I wish I hadn't come here this weekend. I want to go home, I want to see my boys; I want to go back twelve months, before my husband became a selfish, home-wrecking bastard who ruined my life and destroyed everything we had worked so hard for all those years.

'I've been living a nightmare,' Toni says quietly, still refusing to look at me. 'I've had to take loans out on the business. I've...' Her words fade to silence for a moment. 'I've been desperate. I had no idea who was doing this to me. I've been worried that someone was following me.' She shakes her head, her jaw clenched so tightly that it freezes her face. 'I even confided in you. I told you I thought I might have a stalker. No wonder you were so keen to find out more. How could you do this to me, Claire? You're one of my closest friends. Were.'

Holly is forcing back tears. 'Where's all the money gone?'

'You know where it's gone,' I tell her, incredulous. She surely can't believe that I have just squandered it frivolously, spending it on a whim like a child on pocket-money day. 'The house. I was trying to keep a roof over my kids' heads.'

'With no thought about the impact on mine?' Toni looks at me now, the sadness in her eyes replaced with a fiery rage. 'You've got no idea what you've put me through, have you?'

'It got out of control,' I admit. 'I never meant things to go this far.'

'You could have gone to Martha,' Holly says. 'She would have helped you, you know that. There were other options.'

'Martha?' I laugh bitterly, the sound echoing in the silence that follows her name.

I could never have gone to Martha; it would have been begging. But I know what that makes me, and I've lived with the knowledge for months now: I chose to blackmail a friend rather than be reduced to asking for help from another who I have resented for far too long. One I have at times been insanely jealous of.

'What stopped you?' Toni asks. 'Pride?' She shakes her head before turning to the window. The curtains are pulled back, the night that lies beyond them a black sheet that hangs in front of us, cutting us off from the outside world.

We're not going to get out of here in the morning; that much seems a fact now. I will have to face the repercussions of what I have done again tomorrow, in the cold light of day, presumably with the added judgement of all the others.

'But you weren't too proud to resort to blackmail,' she adds.

Holly thrusts the note into my hand, wanting to rid herself of it. 'I just can't believe this.'

'I—'

She turns on me, advancing like a predator primed for attack, and I think for a moment that she is going to hit me. She looks nothing like herself. 'I don't want to hear it, Claire,' she snaps, too close to my face, backing me into a corner. 'I know you've been having problems, and you know I've always been there for you, but this is just unbelievable. I would never have thought you could do this to one of us. The weekend's over – we should all just go to bed.'

'Why did you bring it here with you?' Toni speaks up.

'What?'

'The note. Why did you bring it here?'

I was going to post it before picking Holly up yesterday; I meant to stop at the postbox, but something held me back. It was going to be the last one, I had promised myself that. I needed more – I still need more if I have any chance of keeping my sons in the only home they have ever known – but I was going to find another way to get it. I stuffed the note into the suitcase, meaning to hide it, not thinking for a moment that someone would go through my things. I should have destroyed it yesterday, but it is too late now to think of what might have been done differently if I could go back and change what has happened.

'I don't know. It was the last one, Toni, I promise. I know you won't believe me, but I wanted it to end. I wish it had never started.'

It could only have been Toni who had gone looking for it, but if that had been the case, she must have had her suspicions before this weekend. What were all those conversations about, by the poolside and in the kitchen, when she seemed to confide in me, treating me as though the friendship between us had grown over this weekend? Was it just a plan to catch me out, to ease me into a false sense of security so that I might slip up and offer some clue that I was the person behind the blackmail notes?

I am not proud of what I have done, nor of what I have become. Yet nobody here has addressed what is written in the note in my hand: the threat to tell Holly the secret Toni has been keeping. She must realise that a secret worth spending so much money to keep is a secret that Toni has never wanted to see come out into the light.

'You already knew it was me, didn't you?' I ask. 'Or you must have suspected, at least.'

Toni looks to Holly, who is still standing near the door. Realising that her world might blow apart in the next few moments, she backs down. 'Let's not do this now. No one's in a fit state at the moment.'

'Me, you mean?'

'Claire, please.'

'All the conversations we've had this weekend,' I say, feeling myself grow jittery with an ironic sense of betrayal. 'All those things you said by the pool and when we were in the kitchen last night. Trying to get me to pass opinion on Georgia, about what we all think of her. All that talk of something terrible you couldn't tell anyone about. Were you just trying to catch me out?'

'It had to be someone who knew me, didn't it?' she says quietly, in what I sense is a calm before the storm. 'I just didn't want to believe that it could be any of you.'

There is more she means to say but can't – more implied by her words. If she knew it must be one of us blackmailing her, she had also realised one of us knew her secret. She has known for months now that the truth is a ticking time bomb, and once it explodes, there will be too many shattered pieces for our friendships to ever be reconstructed.

We are both looking to Holly now, each of us waiting for her to ask the inevitable. She allows us to stand here in this awful silence, making us suffer for our lies and our secrets, eking out our guilt and shame. What could I have done differently all those years ago? I had no proof of anything, only a nagging suspicion that I knew was so much more than that.

'I don't think I can take much more,' she says, pressing her fingertips to her eyelids. Her voice is different now, broken; the fire that drove her anger just moments ago has been snuffed out, replaced with a fizzled air of tangible dejection, so potent that I might breathe it in. She looks suddenly vulnerable, frail and so much younger; I think that if I was to push her, she would fall as though weightless. This can't be about the blackmail. She doesn't know anything. Yet. Why does she claim she can't take much more? What else has happened?

'Tell me what?' she finally says. She gestures to the note in my hand. '"I will tell Holly your secret." What didn't you want me to know?'

I can't watch when Toni cries. I remember the first time I ever saw my father cry – I was eleven years old. Until then, I'd believed that men weren't capable of tears. None of the men in my family were the emotional type, all raised to believe that too much evidence of feeling was a sign of weakness. My grandfather's death was the first revelation of a truth that until then had been hidden from me, when I saw the destruction that repressed emotions were capable of wreaking.

Like the cliché that our marriage has become, I married a man just like my father. A stiff upper lip in all times of crisis, because showing emotion is a form of weakness, and admitting fault even more so. Never apologise, never explain. Even now, with our finances and our marriage on the edge of ruin, Gareth remains impassive, as though all our problems will just resolve themselves somehow if he just remains reserved enough. Perhaps his detachment is a form of self-preservation, but it is not the lesson I want my sons to be taught.

Now, I wonder whether the same method of self-preservation is true of Toni. She has remained stoic at times when the rest of us would have fallen apart. She has faced adversity with silent determination, rarely voicing her feelings or giving undue attention to any sense of unfairness. She is one of my closest friends – I still want to hold on to this belief, in spite of all my crimes against her – yet she has always remained a closed book in so many ways, keeping entire portions of her personality withdrawn. I always believed her to be a deep thinker – spiritual, even – yet now it seems that her reserve was nothing more than a shield behind which she was able to hide her secrets; from Holly, at least.

'This is going to kill us,' Toni says, her voice weakened to a quiver, her words focused on me. I have no idea whether she means her and me, or all three of us. The truth is that there are likely to be even wider, more far-reaching consequences.

'You should have told her at the time,' I say.

'Told me what?' The words erupt from Holly. Toni and I are silenced by her outburst, neither of us willing to offer up the truth. At her sides, her hands have balled into fists. I have never seen her this way, as though her anger might morph into violence.

Toni moves towards her, and despite her anger, Holly allows her to take her hand. 'I've always wanted to tell you. I've been a coward, I know that. I was so scared of losing you, Holly. We needed each other. You were one of my closest friends, you always have been. I thought I could make it work; I thought over time I might start to forgive myself, but I couldn't, not really—'

'Just spit it out,' Holly says, cutting short Toni's tirade of excuses. This time her words are hesitant, reluctant; I wonder whether she already knows what she is about to hear.

The tears that roll down Toni's cheeks are fat and unashamed. A look passes between them, and Holly must see it there in her eyes, where all truths are eventually exposed.

'It's about Joseph,' Toni says.

Holly shakes her head. Says nothing.

'Georgia.'

Her daughter's name is all that Toni is able to manage. Her eyes plead with Holly's through a cascade of tears.

Holly shakes her head again, her own eyes filling now. 'No.'

'I wanted to tell you,' Toni claims, the words spilling out of her. 'There were so many times I wanted to, but I knew it would ruin us, all of us.'

Holly steps back and takes a deep breath, unable to look at Toni any longer. 'You knew?' she says, turning to me. 'All this time, you knew?'

'Holly...'

She turns to leave, and when I reach for her arm to stop her, she shoves me away. 'Stay away from me,' she says through her tears. 'Both of you.'

TWENTY-SIX

Holly

This is all I know now: everything is a lie. For almost two decades I have been mourning my first love, my son's father; the life I might have had if only neither of us had gone to the party that night. I have been living a half-life, tangled in guilt and regret, blaming myself for what I said and for what came after, taunting myself with all the might-have-beens. I loved him. He loved me. We were going to be happy together, no matter what was said that night.

In my head, I killed him. I might as well have been the person driving the car that hit him.

Joseph was a good person, a loving boyfriend, a doting father.

He was a liar, a cheat, a user.

How different the past nineteen years of my life might have been if only I had known the latter to be true. The grief of loss would still have been a dark cloud over me, but the relentless guilt with which I battered myself might have been eased by the knowledge that he wasn't the person I had thought him. In all those years I have tortured myself, there were people who could have eased my guilt and relieved a little of the burden I was carrying, the same people who watched my agony knowing that I was grieving a lie. All lying to protect themselves. My friends.

Claire might have let me know that Joseph was a cheat. I've no idea how she knew about him and Toni, but however she found out, she might have spared me a portion of my suffering by telling me. Toni might have done the same, had she only found the courage to admit what she had done. Might our friendship have survived somehow if she had told the truth? Probably not. And for this alone, I understand why she kept the knowledge of Georgia's paternity to herself.

And then there is Martha. There is Suzanne. I think of her, just along the landing – a stranger. I can't yet begin to process what she didn't tell me – what she didn't need to tell me – because I know that once I do, I will fall apart. Like a child with her fingers stuck in her ears, I push the sound of it to the back of my mind, pretending I can't hear it. If I ignore it for long enough, perhaps it will go away. Maybe the truth can be undone somehow, and we might go back in time and rewrite history.

After Joseph's death, the police showed interest in an unnamed young woman no one had been able to identify. Joseph had been seen engaged with her in what someone had described as a 'tense conversation', whatever that meant, and though appeals had been put out for this mystery girl to come forward, she was never identified. Of course, I had thought about her. In those first few months that followed his death, I obsessed over who this girl might be, imagining all manner of scenarios in which she and Joseph had ended up arguing. I always brought myself to the same conclusion: that whoever had reported this 'tense conversation' to the police had been misled in some way. They'd had too much to drink; their perception of the situation had been distorted. They were wrong. It was nothing.

Tell yourself something enough times and it eventually becomes the truth.

Martha could have told the police about 'Annie'; if she had, the truth of what Joseph had allegedly done to her that night might have come to the surface. But it wouldn't have, would it? He wasn't like that. Suzanne is a liar. She has done nothing but tell lies. Either way, she or Martha could have told me the truth, and in doing so, they might have saved me from almost two decades of guilt and self-torture. I linger on Suzanne's claim, trying to picture how it might have happened. I can't: my brain won't allow me to. It isn't Joseph. He didn't do it.

And yet he wasn't himself that evening; I knew it before we left my parents' house together. He was aloof and distant, detached from me and from Caleb, barely glancing at our baby son. We had been arguing quite a bit those previous weeks, bickering over silly day-to-day things, but my mum had reassured me that this was normal, this was what happened when you had a newborn. We were young; the pressure was heightened. Things would settle, she said.

The day of the party was the first time I had been on a night out since Caleb had been born. He was eight months old and I was still exhausted, those first months a blur of hormones and sleeplessness. I hadn't been in the mood to go to a party, but my parents had assured me that Caleb would be fine and that it would be a good thing for me to take a break and be a teenager again for a few hours. They didn't want me to lose touch with my friends or with myself. They were capable. Everything would be fine. And they were right, in a sense. Caleb, at least, was fine.

It was a house party; the parents of a boy in our year group had gone away for the weekend to a wedding somewhere.

Things escalated quickly, far more people turning up than had been invited, and by 10 p.m. the alcohol was flowing freely and a neighbour had already called the police to complain about the noise. I had a couple of drinks, but I knew that would be my limit – Caleb never slept through the night, and at some point I would be up with him. Joseph had been staying with us most nights since Caleb was born, my parents more supportive than I could ever have imagined they might be, and though he would often get up to settle his son, more often than not Caleb would continue to cry, finally calming only after I had rocked and soothed him.

Joseph was different that night. It was the drink, it must have been; there was something altered in him, things leaving his mouth that he had never said before. It was all getting too much, he said. He was tired, he couldn't think straight; he didn't know whether he could do this any more. We argued in the bathroom. Afterwards, the police wanted to know what we had argued about. They wanted to know whether Joseph seemed in a frail state of mind, the insinuation that he might have walked out in front of that car deliberately hanging unspoken in the air between us. But he would never have done that. Despite all the things he had said – despite what I had said to him – he was walking back home to us that night.

Toni was there at the party – we were all there. I would have known if something had been going on, wouldn't I? I would have noticed a look, behaviour that seemed unusual; I would have sensed that there was something between them that hadn't been there before. But would I have? I was exhausted, distracted; all my thoughts were with Caleb, with whether I was a good enough parent or if I would fail him before we had really been given a chance to begin. Joseph loved me. He loved us, our new family. Yes, we were young, but we were solid; we always had been. Right up until we weren't.

I told him to go. I told him that if he wasn't sure we were

what he wanted, he should leave and go back to his parents'. A couple of people overheard details of our argument, details that found their way to the police after Joseph died. We were tired and under pressure. The local press portrayed us as some kind of Romeo and Juliet couple, love's young teenage dream ripped apart by tragedy. Our story was a gift for all the Somerset journalists eager for a heart-rending front-page headline that would sell newspapers.

But now, a worse truth hits me, something so perverse and sickening that it raises bile in my throat, choking me. Amid all the pain and shock of this evening's revelations, the thought of it has somehow eluded me. And now it threatens to kill me with its violence. Georgia and Caleb. Toni obviously doesn't know about them, or she would have put a stop to the relationship.

Oh God, this will kill them. Neither of them has any idea what they have been doing.

TWENTY-SEVEN

Claire

Zoe is snoring softly on the far side of the room, oblivious to all the drama that has ensued. It seems unfair that she is able to just switch off like this while I lie here denied any kind of rest, mental or physical, and for a moment I consider reaching for my pillow, imagining it held over her face, my hands pressing down upon her until her lungs give out. The thought scares me. This isn't me. This is the alcohol. It's the medication. It isn't me.

It is everything that has happened tonight.

After Holly left us, I stayed in Toni's room for a while, both of us stunned into a silence that managed to wreak an almost physical pain. No one can ever know what the future holds, but for us I fear the worst is still to come, the exposure of tonight's revelations the turning point that will lead us to the end. Things will never be the same again. Everything is ruined.

'I'll pay you back every penny,' I eventually said.

All Toni replied with was 'How?'

And she is right; I have no idea how I will repay her. I gave it no thought when I made this absurd statement, pushing the details to the back of my mind. But I will pay her back, somehow. I must. And I must repay Holly too, if I can find a way to do so.

'You tried to set me up earlier, didn't you?' Toni said accusingly. 'During that game. "Never have I ever been unfaithful."'

The question wasn't intended to catch Toni out; it was meant for Zoe, but I couldn't tell Toni that, not without explaining about Zoe's involvement with Aaron. And then I would have had to include Georgia. These are not my secrets; they are not for me to reveal. Toni hates me enough without me causing more disruption, and so I left her alone, resolute that whatever other secrets are exposed tonight, they will not come from me.

My phone has stayed on the bed beside me, where I have unlocked it every few minutes for the past hour, returning reluctantly to the photograph Georgia took of me in the kitchen earlier this afternoon. Took, and then posted on the internet. If any senior member of staff at the school sees this, I could lose my job. I'll face a disciplinary at the very least. I will be publicly humiliated, shamed by something I know to be a lie. We will definitely lose the house then, and no other school will ever employ me.

And if Gareth sees it, he will never believe that what the photograph depicts was truly innocent. Things are so bad between us now that should it come to divorce proceedings, I wouldn't put it past him to use the photograph as a claim of infidelity against me, trying to shadow his own indiscretions by accusing me of being the guilty party. Perhaps he will be believed. One look at this photograph and the worst will be assumed. It is out there already, let loose on the internet. The worst will have already been assumed.

A feeling of powerlessness hits me over the head, pins me to the bed, tries to suffocate me. I can't handle it. This isn't how I do things. My entire life has been ripped from beneath me and I have no control over any of it. Gareth has ruined everything we've worked for. We could lose the house. The children will lose their home. It has made me someone I never thought I could be, made me behave in ways I would never have thought possible, though maybe it was me all along; perhaps all it took was something to slide, some shift in focus for me to lose my grip and become the person I really have always been. I knew the truth about Georgia's paternity, didn't I?

I take one last look at the photograph before locking my phone, its screen fading into darkness. Then I get out of bed, my limbs leaden with alcohol and exhaustion, and pull on the robe that Martha gave me, pulling it tightly once again to keep out the chilly bite of the night.

I need to speak to Georgia. I need to get her to take that photograph down.

I am not sure what time it is – 1.30, maybe 2 a.m.? Morning is now only a few hours away. The alcohol and the Xanax are causing a riot in my brain, pounding at my head with a dull repetitive beat that might drive me insane if I don't find a way to escape it. I just want to sleep – I want to drift into blissful dreams and wake to find that I have remained in one, a place in which everything looks different in soberness and daylight – but I know the hope is futile. There is no sleep to be had. There is no recovery from this.

At Toni's room, I linger at the doorway, listening for signs that either she or Georgia might be awake. How can any of us sleep after what has happened tonight, and how will any of us be able to face each other in the morning? I hear nothing, so I push the handle down gently. The room is darker than the landing and it takes a moment for my eyes to adjust. Toni is lying in the centre of the double bed, the duvet pushed away from her; her legs must be cold, exposed to the chill of the night air. Georgia isn't here.

Downstairs, I enter every room in turn, expecting to find her sitting in a corner somewhere, scrolling her phone, the thing so attached to her palm that she might as well have it surgically stitched there. I go into the kitchen last; she isn't here, but the door to the spa building is open, and there is a light on in the pool room. Music is playing, quiet and repetitive, the song lyrics inaudible as I follow the sound.

Georgia is in the pool room, lying on a lounger. Her phone rests beside her, its screen lit. She turns her head when she hears my footsteps, her expression impassive at the sight of me. Her eyes are unnaturally dark, her pupils dilated.

'Claire,' she says – the first time I think she has said my name all weekend. 'Come and sit down.' She pats the side of the lounger as though beckoning an obedient pet. Her head lolls to one side before she rights herself sharply, the movement awkward and rigid, something almost robotic in her actions.

'Have you been drinking?'

Her head snaps up and her eyes narrow as they land upon my face. I have given away that I know too much.

'You should take it easy,' I say, trying to cover my tracks.

'What's my mother told you?' She twitches when she speaks, an involuntary pull at her cheeks that makes it look as though she is chewing the inside of her face. She was doing this earlier, when we were all in the living room together, yet now the movements seem more erratic, as though she has no control over them. She flips her legs from the side of the lounger so that she is facing me.

'Nothing,' I tell her.

'Yeah, right. She's obviously been talking to you about me.'

She is wearing her mother's robe, the one Martha bought her, Toni's name printed in pink lettering at her chest, right where her heart is. She looks suddenly so young, in spite of everything.

'Whose drink were you going to spike earlier?'

She eyes me defiantly, but says nothing.

'I saw you. When you were with Suzanne. You were going to spike one of us, weren't you? What was it?'

'Mind your own business.'

'Listen to me, Georgia. Your mother might be okay with you speaking to her like that, but I'm not. This was supposed to be Holly's weekend, but you've somehow managed to sabotage it. Why are you even here? Is this about Zoe?'

She puts her phone into her robe pocket, then stands and looks at me without saying anything, a sneer twisting at her mouth. I could strangle her, I think, the thought fleeting and momentary, nonetheless catching me off guard with its unexpectedness and its venom.

'This is interesting,' she says with a smirk. 'Claire does have a personality after all.'

'Don't push me, Georgia.'

'Or what?' she says, a hand flying to her mouth, mocking me once again. 'Oh no. Will you put me on the naughty step?'

'What's your problem with Zoe?' I ask, trying to ignore the way in which she goads me, making me feel eleven years old again, alone with the most vicious of the school bullies. I think about Aaron's car earlier, Zoe getting out of it in the lane. 'You know, don't you?'

'Know what?'

I don't want to say it, in case I've got something wrong, or in case she doesn't know after all. 'You know about them,' is all I say, careful not to give any detail away.

She eyes me suspiciously, her left temple twitching. 'You know?' Her voice cracks, and I feel myself tense as her composure starts to wobble, the hard edges she has worked so hard to maintain now softening as she looks at me, waiting for a response. I wasn't expecting this. I don't know how to deal with it or what to do. My head pounds and the room is spinning; I should have gone to bed earlier, while I had a chance. Whatever reason Georgia has for being so upset about an affair between Zoe and Aaron, I am not the right person to help her with it.

'He told me he loves me. But all the time he was with her.'

For a moment, I can't speak. There is a rush of blood to my head, loud and surging, a wave that crashes over my brain and drowns out every other thought. Aaron has been sleeping with Georgia. Aaron has been having sex with the eighteen-year-old daughter of one of Holly's closest friends. Georgia is pregnant. God, she is pregnant.

The thought brings with it another surge of sickness, my stomach flipping, the alcohol in my system burning through me. Bile rises in my throat and Georgia looks at me with disgust, her face twisted at the prospect that I might throw up in front of her. Her features seem to be twitching again, but I can't be sure whether it is her or me, whether the chemicals flooding my system are distorting what's in front of me.

'I'm fine,' I manage, putting a hand to my chest. 'I just... Who are you talking about?'

She exhales sharply. 'Caleb,' she says, her voice wobbling on his name. 'Who are *you* talking about?'

Caleb. The video last night. Zoe's reaction. Not Aaron, but Caleb. The car. Aaron's car. But not Aaron driving it.

'She's, like, thirty or something. What is she, some kind of pedo?'

There is a hot rush of blood to my head. 'I didn't know,' I tell her, nausea swelling in my stomach. This can't be happening. Not Georgia and Caleb. No. God, not this. Now, even the thought of her with Aaron seems less of a disturbing prospect. 'I promise you, no one knows. No one knew you were seeing Caleb.'

I would have stopped it from happening. I don't know how,

but I would have put an end to it before any relationship was allowed to escalate. Toni would have stopped it. Holly will be mortified. They both will be.

'You can't see him any more.'

As the words leave my mouth, so does the sickness that has risen in me. Chunks of lunch and a spray of cocktails flood the tiles at my feet like a fountain, and Georgia springs back, revolted, too close now to the edge of the pool. I bow my head, my guts burning as another surge of sickness overcomes me. 'I'm sorry,' I mumble.

'You're a mess,' Georgia says, her composure restored, her toughened veneer now firmly back in place. 'Don't you think you're a bit old to be getting off your face?'

'Shut up.' I press my hands to my lower back. My kidneys feel as though they're on fire; the pain rises in me like flames. 'That photo,' I manage. 'Take it down. Please.'

She sighs. 'What photo?' she asks, hands raised in mock ignorance, her voice sickly and saccharine.

'Please, Georgia,' I say, nausea rolling in my stomach at the smell of the sick that wafts in waves towards me. 'I've got kids and a job. Just take it down.'

'Maybe I should take another one,' she says, reaching into the pocket of her robe. 'What do you reckon? One more for the family album?'

Everything happens so quickly. I lunge for her, shoving her away. I don't mean it to be hard; it feels as though I barely touch her – I just want to get that phone away from her – but she loses her footing as she stumbles backwards, slips on the wet tiles, hits her head on the lounger and falls to the floor with an awful echoing crack. I wait for her to move. She doesn't.

'Georgia.'

Her phone has flipped into the pool.

'Georgia.'

I step towards her, expecting her to react to the sound of her name, to push herself up on an arm, to groan, to do something, but she is still and silent.

'Georgia. Come on... get up.'

And then I see the stream of blood that stains the tiles, that trickles from beneath her head. Just a tiny trail of crimson that bleeds out into a flower.

'Georgia, please.'

I put a hand on her arm; she doesn't react. I don't know what to do. I look around, fearful that someone else might have seen what has just happened. I put my fingers to the inside of her wrist, searching for a pulse, but I can't find anything. She isn't moving. What have I done?

I just wanted to get that phone off her. I just wanted to stop her from doing any more damage than she's already caused.

But of course no one will believe that. The photograph she took this afternoon has been posted to social media for anyone and everyone to see, and God knows how many people have viewed it by now. I had a motive for hurting her. No one will believe that what just happened was an accident.

She can't be dead. She can't be dead.

But she isn't moving.

'Georgia. Georgia, please.'

I stay crouched beside her, urging her to move. I can't think straight, not when the noise that pounds inside my head threatens to deafen me. Toni, I think. Toni.

I stand and pace the tiles, sidestepping the sick – my sick – remembering it now, and realising I must get rid of it. On one of the loungers there is an abandoned towel, one I am pretty sure belongs to the barn. I use it to soak up the mess, tears burning my face as I try to focus through the blur that my vision has become. I can wash it, or dispose of it. I can say I was sick earlier, up in the bedroom, when I went upstairs after Sean left.

My arm buckles beneath my weight as I scrub the tiles, and I almost slip face first to the floor. Beside me, Georgia remains lifeless. My tears intensify, hot and blinding. I can't have done this. I didn't mean to hurt her. I am not a bad person. I am not a bad person.

But I am. I know I am. These past few months have proved it.

Nothing must happen to me. I cannot go to prison. The boys need me; they can't be left with their father as sole carer, not when he has showed himself to be as good as useless. I am all they have. They need me. I didn't do this. I didn't do this. This hasn't just happened.

Before I leave, I cannot bring myself to look at her. Like the coward I was all those years ago, I turn my back on the truth, fleeing it as though I might somehow outrun it.

NOW

SUNDAY

Claire

Toni drags Georgia's body out of the pool. She is heavy with water, the bathrobe sodden and weighted, but Toni somehow finds the strength to pull her onto the tiled floor. A mother's love, I think, and the notion cuts through me. I try to imagine finding one of my own children here, lifeless in the water, replacing the image of Georgia with one of my own sons, but I can't do it: my brain won't allow me to construct such a horrific imagining.

I try to remember exactly what happened, replaying the argument, desperately searching for its details.

I ran away from the pool room; I remember it now. My brain had erased the memory, wiping clean the moments between the push and the moment Holly's hand and voice roused me. I should never have slept – I hadn't thought I would be able to – but my eyes fought against me, pulling me into a half-soaked oblivion in which every nightmare was real and alive. Georgia returned to me, her face appearing in the darkness of my dreams, a hollow-eyed, bloodstained version, whispering the words from the other side of death.

She was on the floor, lying on the tiles, a tiny trail of blood running from beneath her head. She was inert, lifeless. She was here when I left her, not far from where I now stand. Her body was prone on the tiles, yet now she is in the water.

A voice comes to me, replacing the image of a lifeless Georgia – a voice I don't recognise, begging me with its urgency.

She wasn't dead.

She wasn't dead.

She wasn't dead.

And now it all comes back to me, the horrific recollection of a night that is best consigned to the subconscious, so that I might will it away as a bad dream if I can just bring myself to shut it out for long enough. When I left her, she was on the tiled floor of the pool room, inert beneath the spotlights. She had hit her head – I had seen her hit her head – but that didn't mean the fall had killed her. It didn't mean *I* had killed her.

I panicked, assuming the worst, as I always do. I checked for a pulse, but I didn't really know what I was doing; I might have been looking in the wrong place, my fingertips failing to meet with the correct point. She had hurt herself, but that didn't mean she had been killed. She had somehow ended up in the water.

What if she was alive when I left her? What if I didn't kill her?

The screaming intensifies. Toni's agony is raw and visceral, the worst kind of pain imaginable. I have never heard a sound so intense or animalistic. It is killing her. My God, it will kill us all.

THREE HOURS EARLIER

TWENTY-EIGHT

Suzanne

After Holly has left, Martha and I sit for a while in a stunned kind of silence. There is so much still to be said, and yet neither of us seems to know where to start in filling in the missing details of what happened all those years ago, or everything that has taken place since. Eventually it is Martha who speaks, declaring herself ready for bed. She goes to the bathroom, moving through the motions of preparing herself for sleep, though I know that neither of us is likely to be able to find any sort of peace tonight.

I wonder whether my mother is asleep. She rests in fits and starts at the moment, stealing snatches of sleep that usually last no longer than half an hour. The doctors say it will pass, but it already feels like a permanent feature of her nightly routine. Twice a week I pay a carer to come to the house and look after her during the night. It is all I can afford, but it gives me an opportunity to catch up on some sleep, the rest of the week broken and restless, disturbed by her night terrors and her constant, endless demands. She will be angry with me when I get home. The carer this weekend is a woman she is familiar with, but I have never left her with someone else for this long, and I have never been away from her for two consecutive nights. She will call me all the names under the sun, I dare say. And I will let her, because she is probably right.

She doesn't know about the diagnosis yet, but this week, after the dust of the weekend has been given time to settle, I am going to tell her.

In the bed just a few feet from mine, Martha stirs beneath the duvet. She isn't asleep; I can tell by her breathing.

'Martha... Martha,' I hiss.

She doesn't want to speak to me, and I cannot blame her for that. I have brought the past here with me, resurrecting ghosts and memories that have until now been buried deep enough to be temporarily forgotten. Was I selfish in doing that? Of course. But there is something about dying that makes a person selfish; I am only sorry that Holly has had to suffer for it.

'Why did you keep quiet?' I ask, speaking into the darkness of the room, not expecting Martha to offer me an answer. 'Why didn't you tell the police about me?'

The question is met with silence, yet I hear her shift beneath the duvet, an unspoken acknowledgement of my presence. It is something I wrangled with in the months following the accident; a fact I continued to wonder about for all the years that followed. She could have told the police who I was; it would have been easy. She didn't know I had been driving that car; she didn't know I had been on that lane after leaving the party. The police would have questioned me, and once they had, they would have found out the truth even if I had chosen to stay silent. Holly would have known exactly what happened that night.

And then Martha's voice speaks to me in the dark, her

words barely more than a whisper. 'I knew what it was like to be guilty. I know what it's like to have killed someone without meaning to.'

I sit up, my tired, burning eyes struggling to adjust to the darkness. 'Martha?'

She says nothing more, but a moment later I hear her start to cry. She fights to conceal it, but it can't be withheld, and when a sob expels itself it is chest-heavy and pain-filled, wrangled by the weight of all the words that have yet to be spoken.

'What do you mean?' I ask, but I fear I already know the answer. There can only be one thing to which she is referring. I flip the bedside lamp on and go to her as her tears intensify, and when I sit on the edge of the bed, she doesn't try to stop me.

'I knew that if it was you in that car, you hadn't hurt Joseph intentionally. I knew it was an accident. If anything, it was my fault.'

'How could it have possibly been your fault?'

'If I hadn't behaved the way I did that night, you wouldn't have left. I knew I'd upset you. I told myself that perhaps it wasn't you who'd been driving the car; it could have been anyone. I kept playing out every possible scenario that might have happened in that lane, but there was only ever really one. You weren't concentrating. You didn't see him until it was too late.'

She describes it as it happened, and I wish, despite everything, that I could go back to that night and erase the past, bring Joseph back to life and return him home to Holly. It wouldn't have been long before he revealed to her what kind of person he really was. I kept thinking that I'd tell her when the time was right. But when would ever have been a right time? With every one of those bereavement classes I attended, Holly and I grew closer, forming a friendship that felt more real than anything I had experienced in a long time. Admitting what I had done would have meant confessing to the lie that I had become embroiled in, and Holly would never have given me the chance to explain it all to her. She would have despised me, even more than I have despised myself. I would finally have been sent to prison for my crime.

But that doesn't matter any more. No court can judge me now; no criminal justice system can impose upon me a punishment harsher than the one already dealt. I have eighteen months – two years if I'm lucky. I will go without taking my secrets with me; my conscience will be clear. The process has felt cathartic in a way; necessary, as though I am shedding the outer layers of who I have been and leaving myself with only the pieces I want to stay with me when I go.

'I know you would never have hurt him intentionally.'

I feel a single tear run a course down my cheek, silent and solitary. Martha reaches for my hand and squeezes my fingers in hers.

'The fire?'

I don't need to say any more. She meets my eye, her jaw tightening as she fights to keep herself from returning there, to the place that changed her life all those years ago. Her body heaves with a sob, and when she leans into me, almost falling against me, I take the weight of her sadness, holding her until her tears eventually subside. She sits back, drags the sleeve of her robe across each eye in turn.

'Do any of the others know?' I ask her.

She shakes her head. 'Only my father.' Her lip curls into a sad smile, accepting. And now, so much makes sense. This is the hold he has over her, the reason why she has never been able to live her life as the person she truly is. The person she truly wants to be. I assumed she feared his rejection, but her repression of herself runs far deeper than that. She is scared of exposure. She is as scared as I have been that her crime may be uncovered. Her father is the only person who can keep her protected from the shame of the truth.

'The guilt doesn't go away, does it?' she says quietly. 'It stays with you, eating at your insides – you can't ever escape it, no matter how hard you try. And you can't ever put it right, and that's the worst part. You know it's impossible, but you keep trying to make amends, keep trying to be a better person, the best person you can be; you try to do the right thing in the hope that enough good deeds will eventually somehow undo what you've done, but it can't, can it?'

I wonder why she is telling me this, here and now. She has carried the secret for a quarter of a century, presumably having told no one else. I doubt that even her closest friends know. Does it now feel for her as it has for me, a cathartic process, a healing rebirth of some kind? Has living as the sole carrier of such a painful truth finally become too much of a weight to carry?

She takes a deep breath. 'I caused the fire,' she admits, speaking the words aloud for what I imagine may be the first time. 'The cigarette that started it, it was my fault.'

'But I thought your dad...'

She eyes me questioningly. 'I've never mentioned my dad to you.'

She waits a beat, both of us knowing that neither needs to fill the silence. She knows that I have sought her out online, that I have spoken to Holly about her – that I have followed her life despite being so far removed from it. It was the only way I had of feeling closer, of allowing myself to pretend that the chasm that had been gouged between us on the night of the party wasn't irreversible and permanent. Without her, that night was meaningless. Everything that happened afterwards happened for nothing. Sometimes that was the most difficult idea of all to bear.

'That's the version we agreed on,' she continues. 'Dad made me promise that I would let him take the blame. He didn't want me to live with the stigma of having killed my own mother and brother. My family would have disowned me. Strangers would have judged me. What difference would it have made, though? No one can hate me as much as I hate myself. My dad knew what had happened. He'd caught me smoking a couple of weeks earlier. He'd only recently given up the habit himself, so he went a bit easier on me than my mum would've if she'd been the one to find me. He made me promise that I wouldn't do it again, but you know what it's like when you're a kid and you're intent on defying your parents any way you can. I certainly did that.'

She stares at the duvet, her mind trapped by a detail of some memory she keeps to herself. How much must she remember from that night? Its sights, its sounds, its smell – the horror of what happened must remain with her in full colour, even now, after all this time. Just as has been the case for me.

'He took the blame, despite knowing how everyone would react. My mother's family wrote him off; they said they wanted nothing to do with him. He lied to protect me.'

In the time between meeting Martha in the cinema car park and going to that house party, we had four telephone conversations that lasted long into the evening. I can still remember lying to my mother about what I was doing, feigning college work that didn't exist, using imminent deadlines and 'peer working' as an excuse for locking myself away in my bedroom with the phone. I suspect that on more than one occasion she was listening at the door. She asked me detailed questions about my coursework, in stark contrast to the brief exchanges that usually took place whenever the subject of college arose. The fact was, she didn't want me to be there. Education invited opportunity, and she didn't want me to be offered a chance to escape. As it happened, I did better myself. I bettered myself, and I stayed, already too consumed by the fear she had systematically instilled in me over the course of years, and now tied too with the threat she brandished.

I cannot recall the details of my conversations with Martha

all these years on, but I do remember the way she made me feel. That is something that has always stayed with me. I remember the reason for it. For the first time in as long as I was able to recall, I had found a person who seemed the same as I was, someone who might be able to understand me. When she spoke about her father, her words seemed to mirror my thoughts towards my mother, a sense of entrapment and dependence soaked into every description of their relationship, whether she had intended to make it apparent or not. I am no longer able to repeat back what was said between us, though during those weeks I clung on to her words, breathing them in as though through an oxygen mask, each syllable filling my lungs with a sense of hope for the future. She helped me to breathe. I was young, I was inexperienced, but I already loved this woman, and that love came to consume me.

When she was taken away from me, I found a replacement in Holly, though it could never be the same.

'Your father did that for you?'

'It sounds heroic, doesn't it, when you say it like that? At the time, that's what I thought it was. A parent's unfaltering, selfless love. But I don't think it was that at all. It gave him a hold over me, something I could never break free from. I am permanently indebted.'

'As I am to you,' I state quietly.

Martha shakes her head. 'It's not the same thing. I knew you weren't a bad person. I didn't know whether you'd been driving that car, but I knew that if you had been, it was an accident. Joseph was gone, and nothing and no one was going to bring him back. A manslaughter conviction against you wouldn't have changed anything – it would only have made you suffer. You were going to suffer enough without it. I knew that from experience.'

Her hand finds mine again, squeezing my fingers briefly before letting go. I wish my mother could have been as understanding as this; that like Martha, she might have thought the best of me. Instead, she recognised my guilt and she used it to her advantage. The car – her car – was barely damaged, but the dent to the front bumper and the scratch on the bonnet were enough that had the police been alerted to me, they would have known what had happened that night.

She saw the marks the following morning and asked me what had happened. I lied to her, telling her that a fox had run out from a hedge, and she took the car that afternoon to her brother's friend for repairs. Within days she heard the news of the boy killed in the lanes between Saltford and Keynsham and she read my guilt like a newspaper headline, bold and glaring. Neither of us said a word about it, not until the day the letter came offering me a place at university in Nottingham. My elated heart was filled with the promise of a new life, but the illusion was soon shattered when my mother produced a series of photographs she had taken before leaving the car at the garage all those months earlier, each labelled with the date.

'I don't think you'll be going anywhere, will you?' she said, and then she asked me to put the kettle on, continuing her day as though she hadn't just sliced a blade through my heart.

I look at Martha and I know now that this is it: we will speak no more of Joseph or of Martha's family; after tomorrow, we may never speak to one another again. In an alternative, better version of the past, Martha would embrace who she was that night. At the party, she would cast off fears of her father's rejection, steeling herself for the repercussions she knew it might bring. We would spend our future together, exploring the world and each other; we'd settle somewhere, in a little slice of suburbia we'd get to call our own. We'd be accepted. Joseph wouldn't have gone near me that evening. He'd return home to Holly; they'd raise their child together. Everyone would get the kind of happy ending that only exists in fiction.

In reality, we will leave here tomorrow and return to the

lives we left on Friday, though mine – what is left of it – will be shaped by whatever decision Holly makes. I could tell Martha about the diagnosis now, but I don't. I don't want her pity or her sympathy, and I have insufficient time for the kind of generic platitudes that might be poured upon me by well-meaning acquaintances if I reveal too much of myself. It has always been safer to remain half seen, though now, with so little time left ahead, I wonder whether safety has always been my biggest enemy.

TWENTY-NINE

Holly

I can't sleep. I don't want to sleep. I watch at the window as the snow continues to fall, the barn encircled in what must by now be two feet of it. I am stranded here. Ensnared. Is this how an animal feels when caught in a trap, this sense of helplessness, of having to watch and wait, not knowing when it might be able to find its freedom again, or whether it even will? In the bed at the far side of the room, Caleb has his back turned to me. His breathing is even and calm; he is sleeping with the luxury of oblivion. I envy him that, though I fear his peace will be temporary.

Every time I think of him and Georgia together, the alcohol in my bloodstream rages through me, burning my body from the inside out. It is disgusting. It is sick. They are like brother and sister. They *are* brother and sister. But they can't be. It is a deceit, all of it; Toni is lying, fabricating a history for herself and her daughter where there has until now been a void, a truth that only she knows and of which she has never revealed the details.

I remember what she told me about the night of Georgia's conception. A drunken mistake, that's what she said. A one-night stand. A stranger. After Joseph died, each of us reacted in our own way to the loss. Toni partied too hard, earning herself the reputation that stayed with her right up until she opened the bakery and turned her life around. She had gone out that night looking to forget. She told us she had never seen the boy before; she never wanted to see him again. She never looked for him after finding out she was pregnant, claiming not to need him. The baby wouldn't need him either. They would be fine on their own.

Seven and a half months later, Georgia arrived, premature. But what if she wasn't? We only had Toni's word for that. Was she too big for a baby born that early? I can't remember now. I don't remember thinking anything like that at the time. But why would I have? I wasn't looking for anything that would throw what Toni had told us into doubt. She was my friend. I trusted her.

But what if that one-night stand had been Joseph?

I go into the en suite and splash my face with water. When I look at myself in the mirror, I barely recognise the person reflected back. The past twenty-four hours seem to have aged me, my skin too pale and my eyes too dark. I wonder if grief can change a person's appearance. I think it did all those years ago, when I was forced to grow up quicker than nature intended; I think that back then, time was forced upon me, ripping me from the security of girlhood and casting me into a plaster-cast carica-ture of a woman. We wear our wounds, physical and otherwise: they're in the turn of a smile, the glint of an eye; they are unshakeable accessories that reveal a little something of ourselves and our histories.

Young single mother. Bereaved. Betrayed. But this is not the facade I chose for myself. I don't want to play the role of victim any more. I never did.

I am going to go to the police. I'm going to report what I know about Suzanne, and I'm going to suggest that Toni does the same for Claire. This is no longer a friendship group. This is a farce. We are a charade, a deliberately and intricately constructed illusion of what a friendship might look like if it wasn't built on lies.

I don't owe any of them anything.

When I leave the bathroom, the first thing I notice is that Caleb's bed is empty. In the darkness, his absence is obvious, the curve of duvet where his body lay now flat upon the mattress, pushed to one side as he left it. He couldn't have been sleeping, I think. He has been lying there, awake, waiting for an opportunity to leave the room. He has gone to see her. *Her.* Which of them has he gone to?

I stalk the darkened landing, listening at each bedroom door in turn. Martha and Suzanne are still awake, talking in whispers. This time, I don't linger to listen at their door. I don't want to hear any more than I already have, not while Caleb might be with Georgia. I need to stop them before anything else happens between them.

It isn't true, I tell myself as I head downstairs. Even if Toni did sleep with Joseph, there were countless other boys. What if she has no idea who Georgia's father is? Perhaps pinning her hopes on Joseph allows her to avoid the shame of not knowing. Maybe she's used the memory of him to create a history for herself and her child where there wasn't one, a story that conceals the shame I know she carries with her even now, after all this time.

Downstairs, the house rests in a kind of silence that on any other night I imagine might seem serene. The stale smell of alcohol remains in the air, lingering in a post-party haze, but behind it there is something else, a sourness that's less inviting, the air tainted with the aftermath of the earlier argument that played out just through the doors to the living room. With everything that's come since, my reaction to finding Zoe with Caleb now seems disproportionate. If only I had known earlier that their relationship would be the least of my worries.

I have no idea what time it is, but there is a middle-of-the-night feel to the silent house. The darkened kitchen has a stillness so absolute that it feels as though the world has stopped. For me, in so many ways, it has. I have lived this moment somewhere else, in a former life, and for a moment I am back there, eighteen again. Caleb has woken early, his cries eventually easing after almost an hour of pacing the bedroom. It is 4.50 a.m. My mother came in asking if I wanted any help, but I sent her back to bed; she had done enough that evening. She had already asked me where Joseph was and why he hadn't come back with me from the party; I lied and told her that he wasn't feeling well and was going to spend the night at his parents' house, not wanting her to know that we had argued or what had been said between us. The doorbell rings. I go to the window tentatively, wondering who it could be at this hour; thinking it might be Joseph returning home without his key. We will kiss and make up. He will say he is sorry for what he said, and I will tell him the same.

But this isn't what happens. There is a flash of dark coat, then a man steps back from the door, looking up to the bedroom window. It is Joseph's father. Our eyes meet, and in this moment, I know.

In the present, I inhale sharply, trying to swallow down the memory. I remember what I am doing here, and I go to the door that leads to the pool room. It has been left ajar. The corridor is thick with darkness, but there is light at the end that reflects off the surface of the water. I hear Caleb's voice, and then I see Georgia on the floor. He is standing over her. There is blood at his feet.

'What are you doing?'

He turns sharply at the sound of my voice. 'I just found her like this.'

Georgia groans and tries to push herself up on an arm, but the effort seems too much for her. I watch as Caleb leans down and reaches beneath her arms, easing her up from the floor. I want to shove him away from her, but I can't. I don't want either of them to know the truth of their relationship. If they find out now, after what they've been doing, it will kill them.

'How did she get the cut on her head, Caleb?'

He looks at me desperately. 'I didn't do it.' His eyes plead with mine; he knows I don't believe him. He lied about the drugs; he lied about Zoe. How can I trust that what he says is the truth?

'Mum, I swear to God, I didn't touch her!'

'Georgia. How did you get the cut on your head?'

'Mum, you can't—'

'Caleb, shut up! Georgia?'

She says nothing, just looks from me to Caleb blankly, her eyes distant, her focus removed from us. She is here, but she is not. Has she been unconscious? Does she even know what has happened to her?

The cut doesn't look too bad, but it is close to her ear, two streaks of dark brown matting the hair at the back of her neck.

'Georgia.' I put a hand on her arm. 'Do you feel okay?'

'Did you see her?' she asks suddenly, her voice changed. She sounds nothing like herself, and she looks nothing like herself either, her skin too pale and her eyes too dark, their whites bloodshot and manic. 'Those photos. She's everywhere. You don't know it, but she is, you know. They love her.' She starts laughing, the sound wild and manic. It bounces around the empty room, echoing back at us.

'She's taken something. Did you give her something?'

'No. Mum—'

'Those pills I found in your bag last week. Did you give her any?'

'No! I didn't bring any here, I swear. I would never have done that.'

His eyes are wide and guilty, and when I look at him, I see someone else. Joseph stares back at me, innocent. No. I won't see it. I don't want to see it.

As Caleb eases her onto the nearest lounger, Georgia starts to convulse, her whole body spasming violently. It takes two of us to settle her. When she starts vomiting, I move her into the recovery position, not wanting her to choke.

'You need to go,' I say to Caleb.

'Mum—'

'Now,' I say through gritted teeth.

'How?'

'I don't know; you need to think of something. The police will know you've been here, they'll know she got the drugs somewhere. Please. Go now.'

Caleb lingers at my side, watching helplessly as Georgia is sick over the floor.

'Mum,' he says quietly, his voice little more than a whisper. 'She's pregnant.'

And just like that, what remained of my world implodes. An electrical ringing breaks loose in my brain, the buzz so loud that it should wake the house. In front of me, Georgia continues to convulse, white foam seeping from the corners of the mouth. Her eyes are too wide and too dark as they stare out at the room, appearing to see nothing.

And now I remember. Here, just at the other side of the pool this afternoon. Georgia and Suzanne. Something had been going on between the two of them, and I saw Georgia put something to her lips. What did Suzanne give her?

'You need to go, Caleb. Now.'

For once, my son listens. He's white with fear, and as I

watch him leave, I know that I will never again see him in the way I did just a week ago. Before the drugs. Before Zoe. Before Georgia. And now this.

Georgia pushes herself up, regaining focus as Caleb runs from the room. Her eyes are rolling in her head. 'Don't try to get up,' I tell her, putting a hand on her shoulder, but she pushes me away and stands up, staggering wildly as she tries to regain her balance. I should go and get my phone. I should call an ambulance.

I look at her stomach, any evidence of a curve hidden beneath the folds of Toni's bathrobe. Was this what she told her mother on Friday, the reason why Toni refused to leave her alone for the weekend? It must have been. Does Toni known that Caleb is the father? She can't do. She would never have been able to get through this weekend if she had known that her daughter had been sleeping with her own brother.

Georgia staggers like a drunk, her body still convulsing in a series of sporadic spasms. She is too close to the edge of the pool, but when I move towards her, she steps away. The image of a newborn baby fills my head, red-faced and screaming. A boy. Like his father. Like his grandfather.

'Georgia, careful.'

Her heel hangs over the edge of the pool, her balance barely holding her. Bile begins to spill again from the corners of her mouth, her eyes continuing to roll in her head as she sways. Her body shudders and she steps back, falling into the water. I watch as she flails, getting tangled in the heavy wet folds of Toni's bathrobe. I should get in and help her. I should pull her out.

But all I am able to see and hear – all I am able to focus on – is that baby.

The more she panics, the less able she is to keep herself above the surface of the water. I should be panicking as well, and yet I'm not. A calmness has settled over me, one that should be unnerving, terrifying. I feel removed from what is happening, like watching a film play out on a screen. I feel apart from myself, no longer me.

I watch as her panic subsides and the water pulls her under. She begins to drown, and I let her.

NOW

SUNDAY

Claire

Someone calls 999 again. Martha, I think, though in the confusion, I'm not sure. Everyone's voices have merged to sound the same; everyone's faces a mirroring tableau of horror and panic. I am certain that if I was to look at any of them, my eyes would be sure to give me away. It would be there, magnified – my guilt in colour.

Time has lost all meaning. The world outside the bifold doors is still a sepia photograph, the black night set against the muted white of the snow that's settled and hardened in a wall that encloses us.

'There was an accident,' I hear her saying. 'The pool... yes... I don't know. She was here on her own.'

Toni is frozen around Georgia's body, shielding her. Her head is lowered, her face hidden from the rest of us. I want to tell her that I'm sorry. That I never meant to hurt her daughter.

I want to tell her what happened between us just a few hours ago, but I can't bring myself to speak.

'Who found her?' someone asks.

'I did.' Suzanne raises a hand tentatively, like a nervous schoolgirl at the front of the class, scared to speak in case she incriminates herself in some way. Holly stands near Toni, yet she does nothing to offer her any comfort. How must she feel now, seeing what she's seeing, knowing what she knows?

Beside me, Martha is shaking. Zoe stands uselessly at the door, her eyes focused on anywhere other than the space Georgia occupies. She has been crying, the make-up she didn't remove last night smudged in cloudy circles around her tired eyes.

'What were you doing down here?' I ask Suzanne.

'Getting a drink of water. The door in the kitchen was open,' she says, gesturing back to the corridor. 'I saw lights on.'

'And she was in the water?'

'For fuck's sake, Claire, will you stop it,' Martha snaps.

I need to know what Suzanne found when she came in here. I need to know whether she saw anything. Above all, I want to know that I wasn't to blame. Georgia was on the floor. She wasn't in the water. I didn't kill her; I couldn't have.

Toni looks up, her eyes wild and fiery. 'An accident,' she says, the words escaping in a snarl. 'Why did you tell them it was an accident?'

Martha opens her mouth to say something, but nothing leaves her. 'I... I...'

'There's blood,' Toni says, too calmly, and she gestures to one of the loungers at the side of the pool. There are two smears of blood on the tiles at the point where Georgia fell and hit her head. I didn't clean it up. I couldn't; it was beneath where she was lying. The blood was beneath her head. Either she moved after I left, or someone was here after me.

'Her head's cut,' she says, her voice cracking as she cradles her daughter in her lap. 'This wasn't an accident.' She is discon-certingly composed. This is the calm before the storm.

The silence is worse than the screaming. No one wants to look at anyone else, everyone guilty of some secret that's been harboured until this weekend, some worse than others.

'Did you see her?' Toni looks up at Holly, her eyes boring into her with an unspoken accusation.

'No.'

'This didn't happen by accident,' she says, gesturing again to the blood on the tiles. 'Were you here with her?'

'Toni,' Martha says. 'You're upset, you're not thinking straight. This isn't going to help.'

'Shut up, Martha. You don't know anything. She had a reason for this.'

Martha looks meaningfully at Holly as though apologising on Toni's behalf. 'I can't imagine what you're—'

'No, you can't!' Toni screams, the words an eruption. 'You can't fucking imagine it at all, so just stop fucking talking!' She lowers Georgia gently to the tiles before standing. 'You did this, didn't you?' she says, jabbing a finger at Holly. 'You hate me so much for what happened that this is how you're going to make me pay.'

Her words are so smothered in grief that they're barely audible through her tears. I can't bring myself to look at her. This could have been avoided. But Toni can't be right. Holly isn't involved. No matter how Georgia ended up in the water, I'm the one who pushed her. I still may have caused her death.

If I'd told Holly all those years ago what I thought I knew – and then, later, what I knew to be true – might all this have been avoided? I saw it first at the funeral, when Toni's behaviour triggered a series of alarm bells. No one else seemed to notice, least of all Holly, who was so engulfed in her own grief that she wouldn't have paid attention to anyone else that day. Martha and I were both upset; like everyone else in our year group, we had lost a friend, someone we had grown up with. But Toni was different. Her grief seemed exhaustive, and I realised later, reflecting upon what I had seen of her that day, that she must have already known that she was pregnant.

Then, when Georgia arrived, I saw something that no one else seemed to notice; or if they did consider anything amiss, nobody dared to give voice to the thought. Georgia was too big for a premature baby. I knew nothing of children at the time, but when I asked the questions that Toni seemed reluctant to answer – how heavy Georgia was at birth, how many weeks pregnant Toni was when she delivered her daughter – her answers seemed forced, and I knew they had been scripted. We had all known Joseph was no angel, despite the pedestal Holly had put him on. He had a roaming eye that loved any attention that fell upon him, but I would never have believed it of Toni. Not one of us. And yet, having seen her on the day of the funeral trying to suppress a grief that pushed beyond the reaction of someone who had been simply a friend, I knew that what I suspected was right, and that Toni had brought Joseph's second child into the world.

I could never have told Holly; it would have killed her. She was so fragile in the months that followed Joseph's death that she wouldn't have coped with the revelation that he was not who she'd thought him to be, and so I held on to the truth, always believing that there would come a right time for the secret to make itself known. But that time never came, and I understood years later how naïve I had been to expect that it might. I isolated myself with what I knew, but we have all been stranded in our own ways, all clinging to our friendships in the hope that beneath the deceit there might still lie something that is real and honest.

I wait for someone to ask what has happened, what Toni is referring to when she claims Holly wanted to make her pay, yet no one does. No one is prepared to pry into anyone else's secrets, not now, when there's a risk that their own might be exposed. Any one of us might have had a motive for hurting Georgia; she has upset just about everyone this weekend.

'I didn't touch her, Toni. You saw the way she was behaving earlier in the evening. I know you don't want to think she would, but do you suppose she might have taken something?'

No one expects it when Toni attacks. She is like an untamed animal, wild with fury, driven mad by her pain. She claws at Holly's face, screaming obscenities, until Martha rushes to them and manages to pull her off.

Holly shakes with shock as Martha closes her arms around Toni, holding her until she eventually falls still. Then she begins to sob again, the sound filling the terrible silence that has rendered the rest of us frozen.

'I didn't touch her,' Holly says again. 'But she did take something, I'm sure of it. Ask her.' She points accusingly at Suzanne, who meets Toni's eye defiantly, as though she has been expecting this. 'Earlier this afternoon,' Holly continues, 'when we were all in here together. They were talking over there, by the drinks table. I saw Georgia put something in her mouth.'

Martha is still holding Toni, who turns limply to Suzanne, her earlier fire doused by the weight of her grief. 'What's she talking about?'

'She was trying to spike one of our drinks.'

'No,' Toni says, refusing to believe anything bad of her daughter. 'You're lying.'

'She had a pill in her hand, that's all I know. I asked her what she was doing and she told me it was a headache tablet. Then she took it.'

'You're lying,' Toni says again. 'Georgia wasn't involved with drugs. She would never have done that.'

Because this is what we do when someone dies, isn't it? We erase any aspect of their character that might have been unsavoury, retaining only the elements we wish to remember:

the good, the noble, the honest. We edit history, often rewriting people so they are immortalised as the person we wanted them to be.

Toni looks at each of us in turn, defying any suggestion that Georgia was less than innocent. 'Why would she want to do that to any of you?'

I see the look that passes between Holly and Zoe, who until now has remained at the far side of the pool, silently watching, trying to avoid having to look at anyone, but most of all at Georgia. If her secret gets out, she will also become a suspect. More so than any of the rest of us.

No one responds to Toni's question, the silence making our guilt transparent. Toni shakes herself free from Martha's arms, and when she returns to Georgia's body, I make an excuse to leave the pool room.

'I don't think any of us should leave here,' Holly says. 'Not until the police arrive.'

'I just need a drink,' I tell her. 'I'll come straight back.'

Do any of them know about the photograph of me Georgia posted on Instagram? If they don't yet know, they're bound to find out as soon as there's an investigation into her death, and once it comes out, the police will start to look to me for answers. I need to find those drugs. Perhaps Suzanne is telling the truth and Georgia was trying to spike someone's drink. It would make sense that it would have been Zoe's, if anyone's. I'm not the only one of us to have started wondering whether Georgia came here this weekend with an agenda. Was humiliating Zoe by spiking her drink what she'd had planned when she agreed to join her mother here?

I go quickly, realising that my time is limited, and head straight to Georgia and Toni's room. Georgia's things are beside her bed, her suitcase open on the carpet, its contents spilled in a mess across the floor. I rifle through it, pushing past underwear and cosmetics, checking zip compartments and pockets, but I find nothing. It seems unlikely that she came here with just one pill. I need to find those drugs. Holly has already accused Suzanne of being involved in some way. If I can get the drugs planted among her things, all eyes will rest on her. The police will think she supplied Georgia with them.

After going through the few items in the bathroom, I return to the bedroom and go to the dressing table. Beneath it is a rucksack. I pull out a toiletry bag, open it and tip the contents onto the table: a toothbrush, a small tube of travel toothpaste, a can of dry shampoo. Inside the rucksack, there is something else. A plastic carrier bag. I reach inside and pull out a box of tampons. A chill flickers through me like a cold shiver. Georgia came here this weekend because Toni didn't want to leave her alone. She had told her mother something, some secret that Toni didn't want the rest of us to know. But I knew; I overheard their conversation. And Toni confirmed that my suspicions were correct.

There is a sound at the door. I turn to it, still holding the tampons. Holly is there in the doorway, watching me. She glances at my hands, and her face changes in an instant, the colour draining from it as though a light has been extinguished behind her skin. Did Holly believe Georgia was pregnant? But how did she find out? *When* did she find out?

'Is there a receipt in there?' she asks quietly.

I search for it, finding it at the bottom.

'What's the date?'

'Thursday,' I tell her.

Neither of us says a word more; neither of us needs to. We both know the implications, but where there should be relief, for Holly there seems to be something else – something that looks disconcertingly like horror.

THIRTY

Suzanne

I had realised before Claire left the room that Holly knew about the drugs. She was watching my exchange here with Georgia yesterday, and I think she knew then that whatever had passed between us wasn't a normal conversation. I don't think she truly believes I was involved in Georgia's death in any way, and I think she knows that Georgia came here this weekend to cause trouble. Yet I still wonder whether it was that drug that led to her death; whether by making her take it I am indirectly responsible for what happened to her. Might she still be here now if I hadn't pressurised her into swallowing the pill?

However her death came about, it seems that Georgia got what she deserved. I believe, now more than ever, in the power of fate: that it serves up what is earned and that we all pay for our crimes sooner or later. Lies catch up with us and secrets find their way to the surface eventually. Georgia has paid for hers, as I will soon enough pay for mine.

After Claire and Holly leave the room, the rest of us wait without speaking. It's beginning to grow lighter outside, the sky making its first shift from charcoal to lead, yet it could still be hours until the emergency services are able to reach us.

'Do you think we should call them again?' Zoe suggests, her first contribution since we all gathered here.

Martha takes out her phone and redials, repeating what has already been said – omitting the word 'accident' this time. The response is the same: they are on their way. They will get to us as soon as they can, but conditions are making things difficult for them.

'Where have you been?' Martha asks when Claire and Holly eventually return. It's taken Claire a long time to get the drink she claimed to need.

'She was sick,' Holly answers. 'I helped her clean up.'

Martha studies them both sceptically. 'Very generous of you.'

'Why didn't you help her?' Toni looks up at me. 'Why didn't you try to get her out of the water?'

'Toni,' Martha says pleadingly. 'It was too late, you know that.'

'I'm not talking to you. I'm talking to her.'

'She was already gone,' I tell her. 'I'm sorry.'

'Why are you sorry? If you didn't do anything to her, what are you apologising for? Or are you apologising for just doing fucking nothing?'

Toni's anger surges in waves, rolling in before ebbing again, the relentlessness of the tide exhausting her. She looks hollowed-out and black-eyed, unearthly in the grey morning light that's trying to push its way through the glass doors. When she stands, her hands are balled into fists at her sides, her face clenched with the promise of an imminent tirade.

'I'm just sorry for all of this,' I say, 'but that doesn't mean I was involved.'

'She's a liar, though,' Holly says. 'Tell them, Suzanne.'

Martha steps towards her, shaking her head. 'Not now.'

'Why are you still defending her? We've been your friends since we were kids, yet she turns up and, what, now she's the love of your life or something?'

'What are you talking about?' Claire asks. 'Holly?'

'Everyone else has a right to know, don't they? So tell them.'

'This isn't going to help anyone,' Martha says, panic breaking through her pretence at some sort of composure. 'Dragging the past up like this isn't going to change what's happened tonight.'

'What's going on?' Toni asks. 'What are you talking about, Holly?'

'She killed Joseph,' Holly states flatly, her voice devoid of emotion. 'She was driving the car that hit him.'

For a moment, there is nothing, just an awful suffocating silence. Then a single noise breaks the stillness: a strangled sob so weightless that its owner can't be identified. I know it didn't come from Holly, so it can only be from Toni.

'I don't understand,' says Claire.

'Suzanne was at the party that night. She hit him in her car. Then she felt guilty about it, apparently, so rather than going to the police and telling them what had happened, she decided to join the bereavement group I was going to so she could befriend me to see if that made her feel better.'

'That wasn't how it happened,' I object. 'It was an accident, I swear. I never meant to hit him. I didn't know he was there.'

'But you knew you'd hit someone,' Toni says, speaking for the first time in what feels an age. 'You must have. And you drove off anyway.'

'I was scared,' I admit. 'I know that's no excuse. I wish I could take it all back.'

All eyes rest upon me now, and I realise that this is what I want. My whole life I have gone unseen, invisible, a puppet in the theatre of my mother's house, a misfit among my peers. All I ever wanted was to feel as though I belonged somewhere, that I might find a group of people – or just one person, even – I could truly be myself with, honest and uninhibited. I am strangely alive in this moment, the reason for the attention overshadowed by the way it makes me feel.

Claire studies me with horror, her assumptions about me reduced to ash. I care little for what any of these women think of me. I have cared for Holly, but does it really matter now whether she understands me or not? Our relationship has reached its end, having served the purpose I needed it to. Had I gone to prison for my crime, I would have been there a couple of years. As it is, I have spent almost two decades supporting Holly through her grief, picking her up from the ground when she felt she could no longer stand and being the voice she needed to hear when the ones inside her head told her she wasn't deserving of the life she had lived. I have punished myself with more severity than any court or justice system could have done. I have more than served my time.

'How long have you known?' Claire asks Holly.

'Since last night.'

'How could you do it?' Toni says, her eyes boring into mine. 'How could you come here this weekend and drink with us and laugh with us, knowing what you did?'

When I don't answer, she takes a step towards me. Her hands are balled into fists at her sides, ready for another attack. 'You've already killed once,' she says, her voice lowered, and she doesn't need to say any more – the unspoken insinuation fires invisible sparks between us, generating a destructive energy that threatens to ignite.

'You're being ridiculous,' Martha says. 'Suzanne didn't even know Georgia – what reason would she have to want to harm her?' She looks to Claire. 'Have you seen the photograph?'

'What photograph?' Toni asks.

'Georgia took a photograph of Claire with the butler-in-the-buff yesterday. It wasn't flattering, put it that way. She put it up on Instagram.'

Toni looks between us, incredulous. 'Did you know about this?' she asks Claire, who says nothing for a moment. She casts Martha a look so vicious it is clearly intended to wound. Martha has thrown her under the bus to protect me, redirecting Toni's accusation in the hope that she might save me all over again.

'I got sent it last night.'

'Oh my God.' Toni steps back and almost falls over as she stumbles against a lounger. 'Any one of you could have done this,' she says quietly.

'No one did anything,' Martha says, trying to keep her voice even. 'Georgia upset everyone here at some point this weekend, Toni, you included. It doesn't mean any of us did anything to hurt her.'

Toni looks desperately at each of us in turn, trusting no one.

'I didn't kill your daughter,' I tell her. 'She took a pill. I don't know what it was, but I know it wasn't a headache tablet. She could have been here on her own, fallen and hit her head. It looks as though that's what happened. It was an accident.'

Toni rushes towards me, her grief directing actions I'm no longer sure she's aware of. She is possessed with it, consumed. Once again, it is Martha who fights her off and keeps her back, she and Holly managing to grapple her to a lounger when she refuses to be calmed. Her fury quickly descends into sobs, and as Holly holds her, rocking her in her arms like a child, I try to make eye contact with Martha. She refuses to look at me, and just like that, I have become invisible again.

As the others begin to argue, tensions rising among them like flames that will burn through what little might remain of their friendships, I leave the pool room and return to the main house, where I head upstairs. I'm planning to sit and wait in my room until the police arrive, but as soon as I get to the landing, I realise there is something else I should do. Despite all I am guilty of, I don't want to spend what little time I have left in a prison cell. I am already serving my sentence, and I will soon pay with my life.

It is the first I had heard of Georgia having taken a photograph of Claire and posting it on the internet. I wonder in what way it was unflattering, and whether it was enough to make Claire pay Georgia a visit after finding out about it last night. Surely she would have wanted to see her, to get her to take it down before her family or anyone else was made aware of it.

I go into Toni and Georgia's bedroom. Next to the single bed at the far side of the room there is a suitcase open on the floor, Georgia's headphones sitting on top. I search quickly through her things, casting aside underwear and clothing, checking the bag's compartments for signs of anywhere she might have hidden the rest of the pills.

There is an open toiletry bag on the dressing table, but it contains only the obvious items. Nothing to suggest that Georgia was anything other than an innocent teen. Next I go to the wardrobe. There are a couple of dresses hanging up, including the one Toni wore last night. Behind it is a jacket. I recognise it as the one Georgia was wearing when she arrived here on Friday. I search the pockets on the outside, then grope around the inside. I find an inner zip; I can feel the bag through the lining. I take it out. Five small white tablets.

Leaving everything as I found it, I go to Claire and Zoe's room. I find Claire's suitcase and put the drugs inside one of the inner compartments, where I'm sure the police will later find it. Perhaps Claire isn't guilty of any crime. Maybe she is more guilty than I realise. Everyone here has had something to hide, and everyone has betrayed at least one of their so-called friends. But they are no friends of mine. Claire is no friend; I owe her nothing. All I know is that I won't spend my last days behind bars.

THREE MONTHS LATER

THIRTY-ONE

Holly

Caleb stands beside me at the door to the registry office, gangly and awkward in his suit. The original plans for the wedding were called off after the hen party, the church service and the party cancelled. I donated the bridesmaids' dresses that had been hanging in the wardrobe in the spare bedroom to a local charity shop. I sent messages to everyone who had been invited, though by that time, most had already heard about what had happened. The rumours in circulation have been multiple and varied, the police finally settling upon the theory that Georgia had a drug-induced seizure, hit her head on a sunlounger and suffered concussion before falling into the pool. They suspect the involvement of someone else there that weekend, but so far they have insufficient evidence to charge anyone.

Drugs were found among Claire's belongings – ecstasy tablets, the same drug Georgia had taken hours before her death. No one believes that Claire had taken them to the cottage with her that weekend, not even the police. Claire claimed they had been planted there, and it is at least one thing that I think she has been honest about. It transpired that Georgia had bought some ecstasy tablets the previous week, from the same college classmate who'd supplied Caleb with the ones I'd found in his bag. She wasn't the only teenager to have suffered a seizure from them, though the other girl was lucky enough to have survived. Caleb told me he had no idea that Georgia had bought any, as well as promising me that he had never taken any himself. I don't believe him about either of those things. It is difficult to know what to believe where Caleb is concerned; in that respect he is very much his father's son.

The police questioned us all in turn, repeatedly. I told them that I had seen Georgia in Claire and Zoe's room, and that she had behaved suspiciously when I'd asked her what she was doing there. It was the truth. I had assumed that she had been looking through Claire's things, but after finding out about Zoe's involvement with Caleb, it was more likely that it was Zoe's bag she was going through. She had found that blackmail note while searching for something else, and Toni must have then found it among her daughter's things.

The truth is that no one will ever really know the details of what happened that night by the pool. And I have told no lies bigger than the ones I have told myself over the years.

Caleb checks his reflection in the mirror that hangs by the door to the registry office.

'Ready?' he asks me.

I shove my elbow gently into his ribs, pushing him aside so that I can adjust my hair. I did it myself, as well as my make-up, having sold online the traditional ivory dress that I had bought for the original ceremony and replaced it with a simple tea dress that I can wear to the pub for food later. Today isn't about anyone else: just Aaron and me. It is a fresh start, a new life; a chance to say goodbye to the old Holly, the one who was lied to and betrayed, the one who played the role of victim and accepted all its consequences.

'How do I look?' I ask.

'Mum,' he groans awkwardly, managing to give the word four syllables. He rolls his eyes. 'You look all right, I suppose.'

'Thanks,' I say, knowing it's the best I can expect.

I never told him that Georgia wasn't really pregnant. He learned that it had been a lie after the post-mortem and the investigation into her death, when no mention was made of her being pregnant when she died. Toni would have found out in the same way, although she never contacted any of us to discuss it. She must have assumed the same as I did, that Georgia had lied about it in a desperate bid to keep Caleb. Perhaps she had thought that the prospect of a baby would keep him away from Zoe, but I could have told her from experience that a child is rarely enough to stop a man who is intent on straying.

Other than Martha, I haven't spoken to anyone since that weekend. She called me one evening a couple of weeks later, once we had all had some time to process the enormity of what had happened. We were already different people. That weekend changed us all. I didn't expect to hear from any of them. Claire went home to her husband, to the mess of their marriage and the financial ruin he had brought upon them. She must live now with the shame of knowing what she put Toni through, and the fear that either Toni or I will one day report her to the police. So far, it hasn't happened. I wonder whether she will ever be able to pay back what she stole.

Zoe went back to her mother's house, and never returned to the surgery. She took sick leave at first, citing the stress of what had happened that weekend, the trauma too much for her. One week bled into the next, until one morning I arrived to find a new girl sitting in the chair on what had once been Zoe's side of the reception desk. Toni shut the bakery and went into mourning. It is yet to be reopened. I might contact her one day, but not yet.

When Martha called, she told me that Suzanne has been diagnosed with terminal cancer; that she had known about it before the weekend of the hen party but hadn't told anyone, not even her mother. Her condition has deteriorated quickly during the past month. I suppose it now makes sense that she was prepared to have her secret revealed. Maybe she felt she no longer had anything to lose. I didn't know how I was supposed to react to the news of her diagnosis, but despite everything, I wish her no harm. We are all guilty of our separate sins, all responsible in one way or another for someone else's suffering. She made a choice that evening all those years ago, just as the rest of us did.

'Come on then,' I say, looping my arm in Caleb's. 'Let's get this done.'

Aaron is already in the registry room, standing beside the registrar. He looks handsome in his casual shirt and trousers, his hair styled differently to how he usually wears it; an effort made without it appearing too obvious. I am lucky, I know that. All things considered, I am so, so lucky.

Martha was right about one thing: I put Joseph on a pedestal. I created a fairy tale fantasy around the two of us, my teenage brain believing that we were the epitome of love's young dream, but the truth was that I had known for a while before the night of that party that he was far from perfect. I had seen the texts; I had seen his absences. I had noted the lack of guilt. Joseph wasn't who I'd wanted him to be, but when you tell yourself something enough times, eventually you begin to accept it as the truth. He was a good person. He was loyal and kind. He loved me.

'You look beautiful,' Aaron says as I stand next to him. And I believe that he means it. I believe that he wants me; that he wants us.

In the bathroom at that house party, I told Joseph about the messages I had found on his phone. They weren't the first, and they weren't from the same number I'd seen on his phone before; I had no idea how many other girls there had been since I had given birth to Caleb, but I had seen enough to know that there had been at least two. It wasn't the fact that he was cheating me; it wasn't just about us any more. He was cheating our son when I had forced myself to believe that we were what he wanted.

He denied it, of course. I was paranoid, they were just friends; he loved me but he wasn't sure this was what he wanted. He was tired all the time. He was too young for all the responsibility. It was too much, too soon. He felt trapped. He was confused.

After leaving the party, I didn't go straight home. I waited for a while in the park not far from the house, deliberating over what I was going to do next. I needed to find out who those other girls were. I needed to let them know that Joseph was no longer available. He had a son. He had commitments. Despite what he had done – despite what I had said to him in the bathroom – I wasn't ready for him to leave me. I didn't want to be an eighteen-year-old single mother. I wanted to believe that what I'd convinced myself of – that everything I believed Joseph to be – was the truth.

Eventually, after sitting in the park for what felt like forever, I started to walk home. My parents' house was along a lane that connected our home town of Saltford to the neighbouring town of Keynsham, and that evening it seemed unusually dark, the few street lamps turned off at some point earlier in the evening. I didn't realise at first that it was him. There was no glow from windows to soften the gloom, the trees that overhung the lane in an archway cutting out any light that might have been offered by the moon. As I got closer, I could make out the dark markings on the road, the tyre treads that scored the concrete.

Something unexpected happened to me in that moment, something I could never explain to myself and that I tried repeatedly to block out in the years that followed. I know that how I reacted wasn't normal. I looked at Joseph, at this boy I had idolised for the past two years, and I felt nothing. All those texts I had seen, all those words that had been written to other girls, came back to me on a loop, taunting me as though I was hearing them spoken by his own voice. My fairy tale was shattered in front of me, replaced by a truth I had no choice but to accept. I wanted to feel something other than resentment, but it was as though a piece of me had been removed, some part of me that had been stolen and crushed, irreplaceable.

I spoke his name, but there was nothing. I crouched beside him and put a hand to his neck, expecting to feel his skin cold against mine, but it wasn't. There was a heat that pulsed from him, weak but still there, still burning with enough energy that I could feel the life inside him.

'Joseph... Joseph.'

And then I heard him groan. He reacted to the sound of my voice in the way that Caleb did when I went to his cot in the darkness of the early hours, an instinctive response to the familiar and the comforting. I saw his fingers twitch at his side. He was okay. He was still alive.

And then I heard him speak my name. It was soft and weak, barely audible, but it was there. He said it just once. A plea.

I could have run the half-mile to the nearest house. I had a mobile phone that would have picked up a signal at some point; I might have used it to call the police. Instead, I did neither. I heard those words that had been written, his voice in that bathroom repeating all the truths he had kept concealed from me, the words being screamed by a voice I didn't recognise. Joseph didn't want us, not really. He was tied to us through circumstance, bound by a responsibility he had never chosen. He didn't want to come back to us. He didn't want to go back to the life he had been living.

He felt trapped, but I could ease that for him. I would show him just how much I loved him by setting him free.

And so instead of going for help, I walked away. I went home to my parents' house and to my son, who I would hold close and protect, alone. Who I would raise to be good and honest and loyal. To be nothing like his father.

But I failed in what I had set out to achieve.

I unloop my arm from Caleb's and reach out to squeeze Aaron's hand. From now on, it will be just the two of us. Caleb doesn't know it yet, but once he starts university in September, he is on his own. I have done everything I can for him, raised him in the way I thought best; trusted that he would make the right decisions when it came to being the young man he wanted to be. But he has failed. He is an adult now, and he must find a way to assuage his guilt, in the same that I have had to.

'Are we both ready?' the registrar asks with a smile.

I nod. I have never been more ready.

It is ironic, I suppose, that I went to that bereavement class for the same reason Suzanne did: in pursuit of a way to ease the guilt that had been haunting me. Through our mutual search for atonement, we formed a friendship, and I suppose this is what stands out the most. All the ways in which the girls had become distant after Joseph's death began to take on new meanings after the hen weekend. Where I'd once seen grief and awkwardness – where I had once regarded their distance as a way of protecting me from further pain – I now recognised guilt. They hadn't removed themselves from me because my pain was too raw for them to manage, or for fear that their own emotions might crack the fragile remainders of mine; they had distanced themselves to preserve their secrets, each scared that the truth would catch up with them.

I lost so much in the spring of 2003, yet during that time I secured my best friendships, with girls I didn't realise at the time would do anything to please me. Girls who would always keep me close and try their best to keep me happy at every opportunity, because they couldn't afford not to.

I suppose it must be the case that liars attract liars, though the only person I have ever really lied to is myself. I convinced myself that Joseph was good, and that we were happy. I erased myself from the lane that night, omitting the details I didn't want my memory to retain. It wasn't me who was driving that car, after all. For years I believed myself a victim, but I am not; I see that now. I don't have to be anything that I don't want to be. I am finally severed from the toxic influences my life has been consumed by, and I feel as though a weight has been lifted.

I return the smile Aaron offers, holding out my hand when he reaches to take it in his. I will be the woman he wants me to be, the woman he already thinks I am. I will be good, kind, honest. I will know all his secrets, and in turn he will be the keeper of all of mine. Most of them, at least. I deserve to be happy. I deserve this fresh start.

Tell yourself something enough times and eventually it becomes the truth.

A LETTER FROM VICTORIA

Dear Reader,

I'd like to say a huge thank you for choosing to read *The Bridesmaids*. If you enjoyed it and would like to keep up to date with all my latest releases, just sign up at the following link. You email address will never be shared, and you can unsubscribe at any time.

www.bookouture.com/victoria-jenkins

The Bridesmaids has been a different kind of project for me: a story set across just two days about an event typically associated with celebration. Although it is fundamentally a murder mystery, it is also an exploration of friendships and the complications that arise when secrets are kept for too long. How long is it possible to keep a secret, and at what point when lying to others do we start lying to ourselves?

Of all the relationships within the story, my favourite is that between Martha and Suzanne. Both are repressed by regrets and both their lives have been shaped by parental pressures, and though they have so much in common, their responses to their situations are very different. Their reunion is bittersweet, highlighting all the ways life might have been better for them had each chosen a different path all those years earlier.

I hope you loved *The Bridesmaids*; if you did, I would be very grateful if you could write a review. I would love to hear what you think, and it makes such a difference in helping new readers to discover my books for the first time.

I love hearing from readers – you can get in touch on my Facebook page or through Twitter.

Thank you,

Victoria

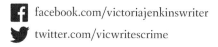

facebook.com/victoriajenkinswriter

twitter.com/vicwritescrime

ACKNOWLEDGEMENTS

Thank you to my editor, Helen Jenner, whose enthusiasm for this book has made it a joy to work on – I really hope that readers share such a positive response to it. Thanks to my agent, Anne Williams, who also championed this book from the first read. To Noelle Holten and the rest of the team at Bookouture, thank you for your continued support of my stories – I really do feel so lucky to do the job I do and to work with such creative and lovely people.

Thank you, as always, to my husband Steve, who has to live with the temperamental me that emerges during the first 10K words of a new book and again at around the 30K mark. I wouldn't get anything done without you. Thank you to the rest of my family, and especially to my two babies, who make every day a new adventure.

I wrote a portion of this story (less than I should have, really, with so much chat and fun to be had) on a writing retreat at Gladstone Library, where I spent a brilliant couple of days with Emma Tallon and Casey Kelleher, women I am lucky enough to call friends. The biggest of thank yous to you both for all your support, for the WhatsApp pep talks and for the brilliant and often bonkers voice notes (that'll be you, Emma) – here's to many more 'writing' retreats and good times to come. This one, ladies, is for you.

Made in United States
North Haven, CT
23 April 2024

51687646R00157